Sister Vision
Black Women and Women of Colour Press

PEARLS OF PASSION

A Treasury

of Lesbian Erotica

EDITED BY

C. Allyson Lee

and Makeda Silvera

ISBN 0-920813-99-2
96 97 98 99 ML 0 9 8 7 6 5 4 3 2

Canadian Cataloguing in Publication Data
Main entry under title:
Pearls of Passion: A Treasury of Lesbian Erotica

ISBN 0-920813-99-2

1. Erotic poetry, Canadian (English) — Women authors.*
2. Erotic stories, Canadian (English) — Women authors.*
3. Erotic Poetry, Canadian (English) — Minority authors.*
4. Erotic stories, Canadian (English) — Minority authors.*
5. Erotic poetry, English — Women authors.
6. Erotic stories, English — Women authors.
7. Erotic poetry, English — Minority authors.
8. Erotic stories, English — Minority authors.
9. Lesbians' writings, Canadian (English).*
10. Lesbians' writings, English. I. Lee, C. Allyson. II. Silvera, Makeda.

PS8235.L47P43 1995   C811',5408'03538   PR9194.5.L47P43 1995

Sister Vision Press acknowledges the financial support of the Canada Council
and the Ontario Arts Council towards its publishing program.

Cover Painting: The Luncheon: © 1994 Stephanie Martin
Cover and Book Design: Stephanie Martin
Typesetting/layout: Jacqueline Rabazo Lopez
Editor for the Press: Makeda Silvera
Pre-Production: Leela Acharya

Published by:
Sister Vision: Black Women and Women of Colour Press
P.O. Box 217
Station E
Toronto, Ontario
Canada M6H 4E2

Table of Contents

Acknowledgements

THE EDITORS AND PUBLISHER WOULD LIKE TO THANK all the women who generously shared their erotic writings making this anthology possible. Also a big thanks to the following for their kind permission to reprint copyright material in this book:

Press Gang Publishers for "You Know I Like To Be," "Getting Down," and "We Pretended She Was a Young Boy" by Chrystos from In Her I Am, 1993; Firebrand Books for "Living as a Lesbian at 45," "interlude," "Dear One," and "Buttons" by Cheryl Clarke from Experimental Love, 1993; Zahra Dhanani for "Cunus Lingus or Chute Chat"; Little Earthquake for "Mother I Love Women"; Jewelle Gomez for "Piece of Time"; Naomi Guilbert for "what i want" and "memory"; Eve Harris for "True Story"; Salimah Kassim-Lakha for "Beloved"; Kalyani Pandya for "Ladoo"; Shahnaz Stri for "Mango."

While every effort has been made to contact copyright holders, this has not always been possible, and the publishers will be glad to make good any omissions in future editions.

Writing the Erotic

I FIRST READ BLACK AMERICAN POET AND ESSAYIST Audre Lorde's "Uses of the Erotic: The Erotic as Power" in 1984 and it transformed my way of thinking about power and about the erotic. Reading her essay became a very personal and intense journey, one that opened up for me the possibilities of human sexuality in all its various manifestations. It gave form and voice to my own erotic expression (at the time unnamed) and to the eroticism of other women's lives.

In the essay, Lorde claims "the erotic is a resource within each of us that lies in a deeply female and spirited place, firmly rooted in the power of our unexpressed or unrecognized feeling... the erotic is an assertion of the lifeforce of women that creative energy empowered, the knowledge and use of what we are now reclaiming in our language, our history, our dancing, our loving, our work, our lives."

I have since re-read this essay many times, using it as a yardstick to gauge my past suppression of eroticism, my eventual coming to terms with it and the final celebration of the erotic in me.

As young women growing up, we can all tell stories about the suppression, the silencing, visited upon us once we begin our exploration of our own bodies — the touching, the talking about.

Growing up as a young African-Caribbean woman in the Caribbean and in Canada, like many of my sisters, I was taught both by word and gesture that the erotic was dangerous. The word "erotic" was not part of the vocabulary I learned. Instead, I heard about being "slack" and about "slackness." "Slackness" meant a certain kind of "looseness," behaviour not acceptable in "decent" women; it was cast at "loose" women, potential "whores," "sodomites" and "man royals" — those who men had little control over or ownership of, those who could not easily be confined by male power or made to bend to male values. Lorde speaks about this misnaming forcefully in "Uses of the Erotic":

"the erotic has often been mis-named by men and used against women. It has been made into the confused, the trivial, the psychotic, the plasticized sensation; for this reason we have often turned away from the exploration and consideration of the erotic as a source of power and information."

It is this power and information which women have been taught to despise and to distrust. Despise because it does not fit with patriarchy, because it does not legitimize homophobia, monogamy, because it subverts male heterosexual hegemony. Distrust because trusting this source would undermine male power.

Yet even as I write this, I move back to when I was a child and the erotic was natural, unaffected and freely expressed. Only later did the natural become staged, and stilted.

My memories of being a small child growing up in a small but urban community in the Caribbean are filled with contradictions. I remember suggestive, sometimes lewd songs on the radio, superstition, homophobia, church-going people, wife beating.

But yes, eroticism was felt and acted on more easily as a child. I played house with both girls and boys freely — touching, feeling, without adult eyes. I can still recall the smell of dirt after a rainfall, recall romping in the rainwater on soaked roads, the feel of the heavy flow of brown rainwater between my black-brown toes. On the backseat of my uncle's Harley Davidson, thrilling to the power of wind and machine. The memories are so sensual. Plum pudding with the smell of rum-soaked raisins. The smell of roast yam, wrapped in banana leaf, buried in the fire earth. The lush memory of Boston ferns along the gullies of Portland. The sweet surrender to the taste of fresh mango, its juices running carelessly down my elbows. The seduction of the girls' game dandy-shandy.... for me, *Pearls of Passion* is a reclaiming of the female erotic in all its celebratory power.

The anthology features erotic prose and poetry by women of colour. The editors are women of colour. We wanted to read works by women of colour. We craved the excitement of reading erotica that was black, brown, red, gold and orange, erotica that came in the brilliant colours of autumn leaves, and we also knew that there were many African, First Nations, mixed race women, East, South and South-East Asian women, who wanted to see themselves reflected and revealed in stories of the erotic.

As Lorde points out, we have not taken the time to explore our own eroticism through our own lenses and, as a result, we have helped to write out of history our erotic selves. Instead, we have been on the front lines in the war against racism, sexism, homophobia, sometimes in our own backyards, in school yards, on the streets. We have been busy taking care of the needs of others, taking little if any time to experience the eroticism living in and around us.

This dismissal of the body is deeply rooted in the constant struggle not to fall into the stereotypes that still appeal to the dominant white Euro-American imagination. We cannot, however, let that imagination govern ours. *Pearls of Passion* takes up where past writers and artists of colour left off. Like their foremothers, the contributors sometimes challenge and sometimes ignore the stereotypes. African-American writers, Ann Shockley and James Baldwin in the 1960s were two artists who explored lesbian and gay erotic life. More recently, many writers from communities of colour have been writing erotica, and there are now a number of anthologies featuring the erotic writings of both established and emerging writers.

Still, there is always that nagging question in the back of the mind: will some of these stories add to the stereotypes about women of colour? There is no easy answer to this question that each writer, each artist, must ask herself. She must also ask herself if such work is influenced by male images, heterosexual or gay.

Pearls of Passion is a torrid and celebratory anthology of lesbian erotica. Open it and you will hear a chorus of women singing body's praises. The voices are varied and joyous, the harmony woven by the common threads of identity and endeavour. These are the voices of women who love women, writers who leave no sense unexplored, no possibility untouched.

This book is not divided into sections, at least not in a deliberate fashion. Instead, we wanted each piece to stand on its own, to offer its own flavour, to give its own pleasure, to feed our imaginations and spiritual appetites. Nonetheless, the pieces about the sensuality of food came together to form what could be a section.

Little Earthquake and Tomiye Ishida open the collection with delicious, sexy poems that promise pleasure:

mother i love women
i am closer than i have ever been to home
closer to the country of my womanself
with its breasts and vulvas and lips
tenderness kissing skin
body meeting body naked
thighs rising to the joy of another
woman touching the deepest sun of my
i

Little Earthquake

Tsuki ga Deta
Liquid sprawl softens and warms
each curve of golden honey.
Tangled black hair whispers
of passionate struggles and
draws me to the tenderness....

Tomiye Ishida

R.H. Douglas' "Sexy Recipes... from the Diary" confirms the connection between food and passion. In this piece she explores her love for the international: "...you know, being a Caribbean woman I just love anything creole, and as an international food lover I also passionately love anything Italian; but nothing I'd ever tasted prepared me for this. A wild combination of spices. Two distinctly different flavours in one exotic pepperpot."

and

"My eager, anxious tongue slipped in and out of slightly salted moisture that reminded me of oysters without the Shadowbennie and hot, hot sauce. I savour the fragrance of both your womanness. My lips, the tip of my nose brushes against the gentleness of your forest."

Effie Pow, Lisa Valencia-Svensson, Kitty Tsui, Shahnaz Stri, and Kalyani Pandya, celebrate the touch, taste and smell of lychee, sugar cane, coconut, watermelon, mandarin oranges, peaches, mangos, strawberries, sweet coconut and coloured rice. Their pleasure in food drips off the page.

In the short story "Piece of Time," Jewelle Gomez takes us to the Caribbean where the tender story of a Black American woman tourist and the hotel's housekeeper unfolds: "Early in the morning she entered with her key. I was awake but lying still. She was out of her clothes and beside me in a moment. Our lovemaking began abruptly but built slowly. We touched each part of our bodies, imprinting memories on our fingertips."

C. Allyson Lee's "Ki-Ai" relates with humour the attraction between a Jeet Kune Do instructor and her student. Her second story, "Aishiteru," is a take-off on telephone sex. Kitty Tsui also explores sex over the wires in a steamy story called "Phonesex."

Patrice Leung's story, "Hey Kids, Don't Try This At Home," takes a somewhat humorous look at what happens between a white, male interviewer, with all his stereotypes of Asian women, and an Asian actress.

The works in this collection explore the complexities and intimacies of sister-love — a bit of struggle, a little pain, but always passionate. The women in V.K. Aruna's "Sutlej Cafe," are

"fighters, loners, renegades... the ones who served as bridges, opened channels, provided pathways...."

The modes of expression are diverse and they range from Carol Camper's humorous short story about Tea Purple, a lesbian sex-worker, to Larissa Lai's tender and poetic musings on love.

The poetry in this collection is always evocative and the result intensely erotic:

> *here where your body ripples in its own trapped pool, washed from ocean onto shore.* Ritz Chow
>
> *without a lie this is the way I want you.* Salimah Kassim-Lakha
>
> *slender fingers brushing the inside of your thighs* Naomi Guilbert
>
> *smell musky rose on my fingertips...* Natasha Singh
>
> *Creamy delight and mutual ecstasy.* N. Sc. Woo
>
> *laughter breaking like glass on the pebbled shore* Naomi Guilbert

...like sucking on a raw onion submerged in juicy...   Zahra Dhanani

Your mouth like boiled molasses moving down...   Maxine Greaves

the new lavender dildo Christmas morning wet as fish   Nicola Harwood

She starts to swim in delight and groans loudly.   Billy E.

And, as always, Cheryl Clarke's poetry continues to be hot and raunchy:

> *Late drinks*
> *late talk*
> *and a perfectly timed split*
> *opening against*
> *sheer blue-sheathed calf*
> *denim desire*
> *rough tight*
> *ass against crotch*
> *seamhard.*
>   Cheryl Clarke

The pieces in this anthology of lesbian erotica are passionate, bold and honest. A stanza from Kaushalya Bannerji's "Love Poems" looks at the source of this honesty: "I could not pretend to disregard/ the pungent onion layers of desire/ unfurling with dream/ or flesh made liquid/ I drank you with each cell/ and skin transformed/ to pure pleasure."

Pearls of Passion is lusty and strong. Somewhere between a shout and a murmur, the writers can be heard insisting: "I'm my own damn woman and / i like all kinds of trouble." Chrystos, "You Know I like To Be"

We invite you to smell, taste, touch, feel the power of erotica.

Makeda Silvera
October 1994

Little Earthquake

mother i love women

i am closer than i have ever been to home
closer to the country of my womanself
with its breasts and vulvas and lips
tenderness kissing skin
body meeting body naked
thighs rising to the joy of another
woman touching the deepest sun of my
i
have birthed a new love away from you
(still longing to be inside)
trying to live another womb
loving you, but i love this more
and losing means i will find
another mother to suckle me
a new uterus to shelter me at night

mulaqat*

with a mirror of breath   you stole my body   from its roots
this urgent ritual of flesh   pulls me into your depths
nomad wandering   through borders of bone   i have no home
but your woman's body   living between curves   of shoulder
and breast   head inside   the temple of your thighs
lush tresses of skin   unfold a secret   lotus into beauty
lover   we have tongues tied   to memory of scars
floating oracles   seeking oaths   of origin and allegiance
shall we cross the waters   enter   each other's bodies
sharing our strengths   birthing a soul   of desire
sung to love   giving new incarnations   perpetual
synchronicity   making the pilgrimage praying
for the sacred union   africa and india

*mulaqat meeting

Tomiye Ishida

Tsuki ga Deta

Liquid sprawl softens and warms
each curve of golden honey.
Tangled black hair whispers
of passionate struggles and
draws me to the tenderness
hidden from view.

Her scent moves me
to touch...

Deliberate... slow, soft awakening.
My hands feel your warmth
arousing a dragon in me.

Fingers lock.

My grip tightens to lift and
pin your arms.
Swiftly turning body
back arched
exposing her desire.

The strength of my yearning;
our moans overwhelm me
and I fall upon you
hungry.
Teeth so fiercely embedded
in skin
I can almost taste your blood...

I want to.

Deep in the valley
her waters welcome me
and my hand reaches
deep inside
to grasp her heart.

I want to howl at the moon;
celebrate her offerings!

Kaushalya Bannerji

Haiku

1.
WOMAN

Body to drown in
Like this I do not want to
Learn to swim just yet.

2.
DARE TO SAY

Now let's touch like that
breeze cloud star stranger magnet
flower of exile.

3.
OTHER (SELF)

Black hair like my own
Brown eyes we fell into like
Love despite warnings.

4.
BEGINNINGS

long time since I left
early mornings before they
woke to our absence

Judith Nicholson

what a dream

if i had not held you
for a few nights and days
i might have thought you were only
a dream

but i can smell your scent in my sheets
and feel you beneath them with me
moving
          moving

if you had not kissed me
with your tongue in my mouth
i might have thought this new taste was merely
fantasy

but i can feel you biting my lips
making them wet
          bruising them raw

if you had not held me
i might have thought you were only a dream

Chrystos

Getting Down

to the bone place where blood is made
and every moon's a mother
your hands & tongue
in me a brush fire I wake up wanting you
Shrill cry of a dawn bird between my legs
memories of your sweet brown breasts
brushing my thighs
You go
where no one
has gone before until I'm weeping laughing
as you murmur in my wet ear
your husky voice like hot blood *I love you*
My hair in your mouth burns for you
your lips nibble my lips my breasts
think they can't live without you
Between moments of you I'm a bird
who flies out of vision
You come
like the first bird breaking open the night with dawn
stars bursting into day sucking you I'm made
a moon sweet with light
Crying in the bone & blood place where you make
me
yours

for Joanne

R.H. Douglas

Sexy Recipes... from the Diary

I'VE TASTED THE MOST EROTIC DISH. A CREOLE and Italian blend of loving that totally took my mind and my body into other dimensions of passion, lust and eroticism. You know, being a Caribbean woman I just love anything creole, and as an international food lover I also passionately love anything Italian; but nothing I'd ever tasted prepared me for this. A wild combination of spices. Two distinctly different flavours in one exotic pepperpot.

My eager, anxious tongue slipped in and out of slightly salted moisture that reminded me of oysters without the Shadowbennie and hot, hot sauce. I savour the fragrance of both your womanness. My lips, the tip of my nose brushes against the gentleness of your forest. My own womanness confronts me, demanding to be devoured, to be consumed, to explode... gently, gently, gently. Tongue in clits, sampling this exotic dish, I've come to realise that it's all a myth, all this ethnic difference shit. Your wetness tasted like her wetness and it all tasted salty sweet like mine. Cultural difference don't come into play when we're in heat.

Each of the three of us bringing our own special ingredients. Mine was wonder and surprise and a willingness to submit. Yours a willingness to share and please and hers a willingness to explore.

You see, I am the `straight' family member, same granwomb and all, you know. I am the one with the husband and children and domesticated image of church on Sunday and woman in bondage. I am the one who heard my cousin say "there's no such thing as being bi-sexual. It's just a sorry excuse for being afraid to come out of the closet."

Saute in olive oil and wild Caribbean herbs and spices. Tender, dilettante pasta served with wild Italian sauces.

I knew I would from the moment the plane landed. I knew I would allow myself to let loose all the nuts and bolts and bars of restrictions and guilt and just be. I knew I would want to make love to you as desperately as

I wanted you to make love to me.

"No expectations," you said, "it is not a condition for love, or for making love."

Okay, no expectations. But what am I supposed to do, make love to both of you?

"We haven't slept outside of us, since we met." But still, what do I do with both of you?

"Well let's not preplan, let's just flow." Right! I smile as I become aware of the pulsating activity between my legs. My clit surely was not a bit concerned with sampling this culinary concoction, tempting me with aromas of excitement that makes my steam rise, wet with anticipation. The moisture flip-flopping of my clit urges me to gaze ahead, seeing us, all three bodies wrapped in the aroma of this exotic ethnic stew.

I smile and you ask why. I always wanted to caress you, to explore your womanness. Maybe because we have so much in common, coming from the same spicy Creole stock, same granwomb and all. And in our lust for passion and sensuality. All this Caribbean wantonness which encircles our sexuality, our sensuality knowing no bounds, we must express it, lest we explode from the build-up of passion. All this female exuberance.

There is an understanding here that we must explore.

The surprise mix of spices. The laniaguiape of Italian blends stirred in with Creole passion. I bubble and bubble, so many tiny explosions, all over me, all at once. Tiny pockets of air plopping and plopping and the tickle of an orgasm creeping down my spine, slowly carousing, coaxing its way down the steep slope of ecstasy, coming, coming, coming with steady, steady flow, emptying all into you, into her, and I rest.

Body memory you call it. Woman memory I say. My body knew yours and my tongue knew all the sensitive places. My fingers did not need the Yellow Pages to curl around the warmth of your thighs. Heh, is that me breathing? Slow and deep, now increasing. Or is it your breath I hear between the pulsating of my breast, nipples taut as your fingers gently leave your tongue, wet and moist with your saliva, you massage my nipples as they stand erect, commanded to attention by the gentle motion of your fingertips. Take them in your mouth, my heart pleaded and my clit agreed, take them, take them, take them. And, you hearing my silent plea of heaving pelvis and breasts raised to meet your lips, respond with tenderness and passion and I come, with your lips on my nipple sucking all my womanness, all my womanness, all my womanness. What can I give you in return for this pleasure? How can I reciprocate for receiving this joy? This river which flows from me, making me smile that I am Woman. That we are Women. Soft and gentle whispers of orgasm or loud explosive bangs. No ranting, raving lunatic pumping maleness and frightening my sensuality away.

"No expectations...."

My stomach lurches forward and I feel you in a lot of different places in my body. Places whose secrets are revealed only to us for we are Women, keepers of Pandora's box, Isis secrets, Queen Bees and Black Widow spiders who mate and kill. We have the secret of our woman power and it is powerful!

Wondered if you would smell different and taste different. But you did not. You smelled and tasted like a woman, like me, when I masturbate and taste my warm womanness off my active fingers. And when I taste my sisters' Creoleness.

Each of the three of us bringing our own special ingredients. Mine was wonder and surprise and a willingness to submit. Yours a willingness to share and please and hers a willingness to explore.

I hear and try to understand my sister cousin say "there is no such thing as bi...."

There is something here we must explore.

Kaushalya Bannerji

Love Poems

1.

I could not pretend to disregard
the pungent onion layers of desire.
Unfurling with dream
or flesh made liquid.

2.

I drank you with each cell
and skin transformed
to pure pleasure.
No one knows I know you.
Like this, hands all moans
breasts like sighs.

3.

Our touch is more than contact.
We create each other.
Your voice in my throat
Your hands in my centre.
I make of myself
Cave, well, womb, mouth, heart.

Effie Pow

She is a red bean woman

She is a red bean woman.
Durian breasts, lychee lips, mango cheeks
sugar cane arms, watermelon belly, coconut tears —
a wetness all over that makes everything
taste good together.
She has sweet almond bean curd heart, cocktail fruit jokes
mandarin orange generosity, rambutan touch,
sweet potato words, water chestnut sensibilities,
chrysanthemum tea crystal wishes,
and salty dried plum nipples to make your mouth water.
And when you hold one
in your mouth long enough,
the revived flesh
slips off its
pit.

Lisa Valencia-Svensson

The Peach Pit

Last night I ate a peach
We were watching some crap movie
on the television screen
"Poltergeist" from the past
loomed large again in our home

I sucked away all the flesh
the sweet juice
hoping to fill my need
my craving for something as yet undefined....

The pit remained
held tight in my fingers
my mouth returned
searching for more

My tongue tested the hardness
the rough outlines
raised up on one side
very much a woman in disguise

I fastened tight
on the two lip-like protrusions
my tongue pressing firmly into the middle
sending shock waves
straight to your core

I kissed and nibbled
at my peach pit
with passion I meant
for a lover

and I realized
late night movies just don't cut it anymore

Sherece Taffe

dinner conversation

girl don't be givin me that look
that "wish we were alone so i could fuck you" look
you know the look i mean
that "i hope we can slip away quickly so i can taste you" look
you know the one that says "if only we could just leave already"
the look that speaks volumes the look that weakens me
puts me on edge expectin somethin
the "i want you now" look
the "how much longer before i can get my hands on you" look
you must know what i mean girl don't be givin me that look
that "no one is watching can't i just lick your ear" look
that "i know we just got out of bed but i want more" look
that "remember how i touched you there" look
the one that says "how much longer will this take"
the "i'm so horny i might explode" look
do you know what that look does to me girl don't do it
girl control those eyes girl put that look back
girl what do you mean i ain't givin you no look girl
but look... what are we still doin here girl

Kitty Tsui

Vanilla and Strawberries

ONE OF THE BIGGEST ADVANTAGES OF WORKING in the Financial District downtown is watching women on their lunch breaks. There are hundreds of them: hurrying to mail letters before a lunch date, buying yogurt, salad or sandwiches, going into Nordstrom's, or running to the bank. There are women in skirts, stockings and running shoes, and women in business suits and high heels. Some wear hats, have their hair fashionably coiffed, or loose and flying free. Some wear full make-up or are totally without facial adornment. To this lesbian, they all bring a smile to my face and help break up the monotony of a nine-to-five job.

I was sitting on a bench in the sun eating a hot dog when I saw her. She was looking at her watch and waiting impatiently for the red light to change. The thing that struck me first about the woman was her hair. It was salt and pepper. Actually it was grey, but salt and pepper is probably the more *de rigueur* term. She had grey hair; it matched her grey pin-striped suit. She had on black-seamed stockings and black pumps, and carried a burgundy briefcase. At first glance, she was to me a very striking woman. But then, I must confess, I love older women and women who wear skirts, even if they are business-type suits.

I continued chewing on my hot dog, embellished with relish and extra onions, hoping the traffic light would not change. Being a shy girl I had no smart ideas on how to delay this woman for even a second. I did, however, regret the onions on my hotdog, even at this distance.

The red light turned green. The woman with the striking grey hair hurried across the street and rapidly disappeared from my line of vision. I finished my hot dog and returned to my job.

I work in the graphics department of a large advertising agency. One of our most successful executives had just given notice. She'd found out that her recent weight gain was not the result of being wined and dined on a regular basis by grateful clients. According to her obstetrician, she was pregnant. Pearce and Pearce Advertising Associates was seeking someone to fill her position.

It was a Friday and a record-breaking hot day. The receptionist had called in sick, something I wished I had been able to do. And though I had a pile of my own work, being one of the only women and the newly-hired staff person, I was assigned to sit at the front desk.

Somewhat resentful at having to answer phones and smile at prospective clients while neglecting my own deadlines, I suddenly brightened when the grey-haired woman walked through the door.

"I have an appointment," she announced briskly, "with Brandon Pearce."

"Uh... yes," I replied, stammering like an adolescent, "your name, please."

"Jayne," she answered, "with a y. Smyth, also with a y."

"Have a seat," I said, playing the receptionist role to the hilt. "I'll let him know you're here."

The receptionist returned to work on Monday, a typically foggy San Francisco summer day. Jayne Smyth joined Pearce and Pearce Advertising Associates the following week.

I have certain rules that I try to adhere to that govern my behavior as a nice Chinese girl. One, I do not get involved with anyone on the job. Two, I am not interested in straight women. And three, women who do not like my dog do not stay long in my bed.

Jayne Smyth is originally from England, as am I, though I was born in Hong Kong. She is ten years older than I and was trained as an opera singer, though she did not follow that calling. We hit it off immediately, finding that we had, surprisingly, the same background and experiences.

I found her very attractive, whether in dresses, tailored suits or designer ensembles. When I told her I was a lesbian she replied simply that we had something else in common. Needless to say, I was thrilled.

Rules and regulations are the cornerstones of society. 3,000 years of Chinese civilization had certainly taught me that. However, being a contemporary woman, and a feminist to boot, I was convinced that some rules were meant to be broken. Early in our acquaintance I found out that Jayne loved dogs. Since she was not straight, the only other hurdle was the fact that we worked together.

I rationalized it quite simply. I was a graphic designer and she was an account executive. So what if we worked for the same company? We were in two totally separate job situations.

We frequently lunched together. We never talked about work. The sexual tension between us grew unbearable. It had been almost a month since she started working at the agency, and lunching together had been the extent of our activities. I decided it was time for Jayne to meet my dog, Meggie.

"We've been doing lunch for a month now," I began, "how about dinner at my place tonight?" It was the Friday before the Fourth of July, the start of a long holiday weekend. I figured she already had other plans.

"Sure. Sounds great. What shall I bring?"

Jane came over at seven. We started with seltzer, salt-free tortilla chips and salsa. Meggie loved her because Jayne fed her tortilla chips. We listened to Billie Holliday and K.T. Oslin. I fixed poached salmon, wilted spinach salad with bacon and crushed peppercorns, and sourdough baguettes. After dinner we contemplated going to the movies but couldn't agree on one. We sat on the couch and petted the dog. This went on for what seemed like an awfully long time.

All kinds of questions went through my mind: want to see my porfolio? Like C and W? Do you line dance? Wanna go for a walk with the dog? Actually what I really wanted to say was: wanna fuck? But seeing that she was from another generation, I thought it might not be the most appropriate thing to ask.

Instead I said: "I have ice cream in the fridge. Strawberries too, if you're not into sugar."

"What kind of ice cream do you have?" she asked, "I'm very particular about my ice cream."

"Me too," I replied, "I only like one kind of ice cream."

"What kind's that?"

"Vanilla."

"Hum, vanilla and strawberries. Great combination. Ever eaten in the tub?"

"Uh... excuse me..." I said, in a bit of a shock.

"Haven't you ever had ice cream and strawberries in the bathtub?"

"Well, as a matter of fact, no."

"Want to give it a try?"

"Uh, well..." I stammered, trying to keep my demeanour.

"You know what Tina Turner said, don't you?"

"What's that?"

"I'll try anything one time."

"I'm not sure I'm as daring as Tina Turner, but, well... what can I say?"

"Say you're game," she teased, looking me straight in the eye.

"All right, Jayne."

Jayne dished out the ice cream into big bowls and washed the longstemmed strawberries. I filled the tub, lit some candles and put my yellow rubber ducks into the water.

Jayne came into the bathroom and undressed me. She kissed my neck and bit my bare shoulders. She unbuttoned my jeans and pulled them off, one leg at a time. She slipped off my socks and kissed the tops of my feet.

"Get into the water," she smiled, "I'll feed you."

I did as I was told, finding it not altogether unpleasant to take orders from her. Jayne fed me strawberries and ice cream while I luxuriated in the warm water. I took the sweet berries in my mouth and licked ice cream from her fingers. Warmth enveloped me up to my neck. Heat rose from between my legs.

Jayne washed me all over with lavender soap. She scrubbed my back and ass with a loofah, took my toes into her mouth and sucked on them. I moaned and squeezed my rubber ducks. She put her hand between my thighs and opened me up to her fingers. I felt the rush of water entering my inner lips as she pushed inside me.

"Aren't you glad you listened to Tina?" she laughed.

The candles were burning low as I got out of the tub. Jayne took a thick towel and patted my body dry. She got down on her knees between my open legs and took me in her mouth.

I'm so glad I listened to Tina Turner. Private dancer, better be good to me.

Shahnaz Stri

Mango

YESTERDAY I WAS SITTING IN THE HOT SUN, MAYBE i was walking and i came upon a small park. it was quiet. no one was in it. then i looked again and i saw a woman. she had long black hair. she was reading underneath a tree and beside her was a blanket spread out with food, mostly fruit. she wasn't aware of anything, she was quite engrossed in her book. i wondered what she was reading. how she had found this place. was it the same way that i had. walking down a city street and right in the middle is this park. the park appears big, but it is quite small, because the map doesn't even show it. it didn't appear that this woman was questioning the existence of this park, as i was. but then i have a habit of doing that. questioning things, little things. things that don't connect. i am always suspicious. this park was curious, though. the trees were all fully leaved, the grass was a cool dark green, and the air smelled cleaner. i didn't feel hot from the sun that i had just left. the sun in the park wasn't glaring. the city does that to sun. makes it mean. there aren't any benches or picnic tables, just a small water fountain. not your standard type, issued by the parks and rec dept. it was like a small tub, all painted black, to fit in with the park scenery.

i walked further, and the grass was spongy. i wanted to ask the woman what she was reading. but it appeared that she wasn't even aware of my presence. she was a beautiful woman. her hair showing different shades of brown to black, by the reflecting sun. her arms were brown, a rich brown colour. the fingers were playing with her hair. a nervous twisting, which seemed so out of place with the scenery. perhaps waiting for someone or something. and i walked closer, trying to find her eyes, her face hidden by the shadows of the tree she was sitting under. her book was propped on her knee. and then she looked up. perhaps she heard my careless steps in this unfamiliar environment. my staring at her. my presence she might have sensed. she didn't say anything. she just looked at me, waiting perhaps for me to say something. but there was no look of expectation on her face. she picked up a fruit. a mango. she started to cut it into thin slices. the colour of it contrasted with everything in the park. its brightness made my mouth water. and i could taste the flavour. its sweetness lingering in my mouth. i could smell the ripeness from where i was standing. i sat down close to her feet and she handed me a piece. but it was only a small piece. like temptation. tantalizingly so near. she watched me eat it. the juice dripped down my chin. my questions of her forgotten. and my appetite was wanting more of this mango, like no mango i had found in the city. like the mangoes in india.

and when i had finished eating her mango slices, i looked up. she was no longer there. and i, i was standing in the middle of a street with the sun beating down on my hot skin, yet i felt cool inside. satisfied.

Kalyani Pandya

Ladoo
(especially for Ruth)

and she wants to offer her ladoo
to place the sweet blessings on her tongue
to hear her lover's name chanted in wedding song
a prayer thick with the Indian accent of her people
invoked with sweet coconut
and coloured rice
and garlands woven with sacred flowers
conjuring her past in Sanskrit
making her vows in her mother tongue
she wants to walk around the puja fire
seven times with her lover

Kalyani Pandya

m&m's

I could not say that it is not
your beauty that I remember   or rather
that remembers itself to me
I could not tell
whether the heat of that night follows me
or if it is I who pursue   still
the shadows of that impossibility   we did not
as I recall love each other that night it
cannot have happened   nor did I
as my false memory suggests   watch
as you revealed your body to me as you peeled
from your waist
the soft black cloth it
cannot be that I held you then that
I touched with my lips (my lips!)
the tender dream that met me there no
I did not love you that night
while "The Unbearable Lightness of Being"
played on   and I surely did not share with you
peanut and chocolate m&m's
it would not happen that way
I would not have lost you
I would not have lost you
I would not have
Lost you.

V.K. Aruna

Disco

BACKGROUND: WHEN RAJKUMARI WAS DEPORTED to Malaysia, she had no time to plan for her return to a country she had not seen for twelve years. Consequently, when she landed at Subang Airport, she was broke, homeless and isolated from any lesbian community in her home city of Kuala Lumpur.

Six months later, she found herself at an old friend's party, fielding questions about her marital status, and replying as nonchalantly as she could, "You know me... I've never wanted to marry," hoping that would end the interrogation. It didn't.

The friend continued, "Well, what about a boyfriend? Met any nice guys over there?"

Across the airwaves, came a warning: "This is a test. This is only a test...." Rajkumari sighed.

The friend noticed her hesitation and teased, "Hey, come on out with it. Who's the bugger? Is he a Mat Salleh?"[1] The time had come. Rajkumari took a long drag of her Marlboro unfiltered cigarette, looked her friend in the eye and said, "I am a lesbian. I love women." She never saw her friend after that, but a guest at the party heard the gossip and managed to track down Rajkumari with a name for an underground activist lesbian group called Jendela, which in Malay means "window."

It took a while but eventually the invitations came — to dim sum, jazz bars, then Saturday-night outings to clubs where women played boys and boys played queens, and the lesbians knew who the lesbians were but no one said anything. Soon, she even found a room to rent, a job interview, a good deal on a car — all through this nebulous network of women who reminded her of the convent school girls she had once fallen in love with.

Then word came that an ex-lover and political ally had been killed in a car accident in the USA and left Rajkumari a one-million dollar life insurance policy. By that time disco was making a fast comeback in many metropolitan cities of the geographic Third World, following the lead of the

USA Retro Age during the Clinton era. Rajkumari chose to honour the memory of her friend by opening a disco, bar and cafe, since her friend had been a disco fiend during the seventies and had frequently talked about opening a lesbian cafe.

A search through downtown real estate properties gave Rajkumari what she was looking for — an elegant office building in the heart of K.L. She bought three floors, located the disco in the basement, the bar on the main floor, and the cafe on the floor above. Each was designed for a distinct atmosphere. On black marble doors at the main entrance she had the name, Scheherezade, carved in brass letters. In front, she posted security officers to keep men out. Soon, within the teak-panelled walls of this private club, Rajkumari attracted a steady clientele of lesbians who had tired of meeting in gay male hang-outs run by heterosexual entrepreneurs.

It wasn't long before Scheherezade earned the reputation of corrupting women's morals. Urban Malaysia, which had long since legitimized the gay group, Pink Triangle, and contended with the reality that AIDS was there to stay, found itself learning to live with gay men. The same allowance did not extend to lesbians. Rajkumari turned to her friend, Alistair Wong, the male drag darling of the Kuala Lumpur gay club circuit. He helped her find contacts high up in government to thwart the closing down of her establishment. Scheherezade survived. Within two years, demand for the cafe grew so much in the general women's community that Rajkumari built a separate entrance for the cafe, hired two excellent cooks specializing in Northern Nonya cooking, set up a reading room, and opened the cafe to non-lesbian women. This arrangement proved successful. She was able to invest money from the cafe into the disco, which she continued to retain exclusively for lesbians. Three years later, Scheherezade remained a thriving operation with customers coming in from Singapore, Bangkok and even Sydney, Australia.

This background is fictitious, but it is entirely probable, and provides the setting for the following scene from a still-evolving short story, "Disco."

Rajkumari's full black outfits were always accompanied by some ornament — a Kelantan silver butterfly with a ruby head, a white brass belt buckle the size of her palm, a malachite pendant on red and black beads, a brocade sash with embroidered tassels.

Tonight she wore a necklet, a simple yet elegant filigree of silver threads woven into strands of burnt copper. From the middle hung a silver pendant in the shape of a mango leaf, with delicate scalloped edges closing in on a single deep red garnet. The gem drew attention immediately to Rajkumari's throat, her cinnamon-coloured skin, the hollow space between her sharply-ridged collarbones, the prominent rise of breasts under a black silk shirt. The moment she stepped into the disco, she felt her nipples harden, and instinctively slid her hands into her trouser pockets to mask her shyness. A cigarette lighter lay against her left thigh, buried in the deep folds of her baggy salwar-style pants. She was grateful for this memento from her smoking days. It had come to represent her resilience. Rajkumari rubbed the sleek enamel finish as if it were a good luck charm and strode under the strobe lights.

At the bar, she picked up her usual — ice water in a long stemmed crystal wine glass. A few customers who knew her enquired how she was, told her how marvellous she looked, fingered the garnet glowing around her neck. Rajkumari smiled, chatted, then quietly slipped to the other side of the room where the pyramid of imported German speakers provided partial refuge from well-meaning customers asking too many questions and offering dinner invitations.

From her hiding spot inside the shadows, she surveyed the audience. The regulars had turned out in full regalia tonight, dykes from other bars who preferred the Scheherezade because it was an all-women's space. But there were also several new faces, young women in close-cropped hair looking tough with their girlfriends beside them, sipping something non-alcoholic. Rajkumari was pleased. Young lesbians in the city were an endangered group. They were safer in her disco than out on the streets, cruising the central market area for night-time companions.

Whistles from the audience signalled that the entertainment was about to start. On the dais, thin and fat women took their places as the opening bars to "Sweet Dreams" set synchronized lights in motion. Annie

Lennox hit the first note. Long lean dancers sprang in the air and slashed the alternating light and dark with arms clasped in amulets. Fat dancers moved like seals in water. The audience clapped to keep time. Lights dissolved from red to metallic blue, fuschia to green. Fog poured into the air. Then, Sarina emerged.

She was the dance leader who had created this performance. Her five foot five, two hundred pound body was lithe and smooth, clothed in a fiery orange wrap-around, the top knotted above heavy breasts. Her thighs were unashamedly bare, a choice that had nearly cost Scheherezade its licence to stay in business. Rajkumari recalled mediated meetings with the Ministry of Culture, the labyrinth of negotiations which had led to a *"special licence subject to final approval."* The struggle was worth it. Sarina's boldness had encouraged large women to come to the disco. Tonight they sat, scattered among the crowded booths and tables — women in saris, kebayas, strapless dresses and low-cut blouses — laughing, flirting, unselfconscious.

The dais trembled. "Sweet Dreams" became Donna Summer's "Last Dance" and the formation on stage changed like a kaleidoscope pattern. Sarina arched and undulated. The audience cheered. She stood feet apart and looked out at their expectant faces, hands out-stretched, her fingers beckoning. And from the bar... the tables... the booths, women surged, not missing a beat, onto the dance floor in front of the dais.

Rajkumari watched... the raised arms, heads thrown back, hips swinging under a mirrored orb circling above. She too had been an elephantine woman until, one day, she woke to the legacy left her by grandmother, aunts and mother, a legacy consummated by her relentless boozing, cigarettes and high stress jobs. The unrestrained athletic energy of women dancing reminded her of vibrancy, of the kind of effervescent life she had once led, whirling in and out of multiple projects, pulling off the impossible by the seat of her pants. These days, she felt as if there was something missing in her life, a sense of fear that had in the past kept her on edge, that, ironically, had also made her feel invincible, as if she were challenging death itself. Rajkumari no longer pranced along the precipice of death, daring it to grab her. She had other things on her mind, such as living with cancer. It was good that she had left the U.S. by the time she was diagnosed. Life among Malaysians was so much saner. Just as death, in time, would be. Still, her dance with destiny had dulled. Things were more predictable now.

The rhythmic fury cascading through the speakers ended. Customers on the dance floor applauded the dancers on the dais. Rajkumari raised her glass to Sarina, their eyes meeting as they always did after every performance, a smile passing between them.

As the CD changed to a slow dance number, Rajkumari left the shadows. In her mind, beads of sweat streamed down a dark oval face, their sheen clinging to heaving round shoulders and to breasts hanging like boughs of jasmine in full bloom. Perhaps they would meet again tonight, she thought, then clasped the cold enamel inside her left pocket, and climbed the red-tiled steps to the cafe.

---

1 Mat Salleh is a Malay term for white people which is now part of the Malaysian vocabulary, across many (mother) tongues.

Chrystos

We Pretended She Was a Young Boy

who had come over to mow my lawn & I'd asked her in
for a cool drink of lemonade
wearing only a negligee of pink peach silk
& a string of pearls
I made her sit beside me on the couch while I told her
how much I liked her hard body & the fine dew of sweat
on her upper lip
& didn't allow her to touch me
I asked if she needed a little back rub after
working
so hard
because I understood what the sun could do to her
body   Heat clenching in the thighs
I said maybe I could help her relax
I laid her down on the couch & straddled her
the smell of me rising up wetting her jeans
I began to rub her hard
wiggling in just the right way to make her groan
but not letting her touch me
She had the dildo on   rubbing her crotch
as I rocked back & forth whispering softly that I hoped
she felt a little better
until she turned over in a sudden movement & opening
her 501's gave it to me hard
while I pretended to be shocked in delicious protests
my nipples so hard pushing out the silk of our need

She touched me without my permission pulling
the pearls until I touched her lips kissing me hard
her thrusts into me her hands on my hips
the lemonade flying across the room
as I bit her neck coming
so hard

for B.J.

Cheryl Clarke

Buttons

I wanted to unbutton every piece of your clothing
which was all buttons
from that silk shirt
down to the crotch of that gaberdine skirt.
My buttons too:
my jeans brass-button top,
my shirt has six shell buttons,
my camisole has three tiny ones.
This restaurant is in my way
when I want to be unbuttoned
and unbuttoning.
Can't you tell?
To do it now.
To reach across the bread.
To start unbuttoning.
My arms so long.
My fingers faster than the eye, and omnidextrous.
Now, ain't that loving you?

Salimah Kassim-Lakha

Beloved

Softly,
your lips take me on
linger;

and I am reminded of silk on silk
as your fingertips
trace paisleys on my skin
chasing dragons
the
      burn
           rushes
                faster

feel desire smoldering

your voice whispers smoke
cementing me
to the present

I struggle to mix midnight colours
to whip the connection stronger
as your mouth surrounds my emotions

press my craving

I am not shy
and as I move
move on top of you

our rhythms touch wind chimes
Travelling

I hear my name through
        sweat
             heat
                   and darkness

Hands tighten on my shoulders
Ache,
Concentrate
and I drink the reward of
        an
                arched
        back

Rising, I transfer salt to your neck, lips

Making magic

fading and sparkling magic
that holds enchantment from the heart
and melts chaos from the hips
Beloved

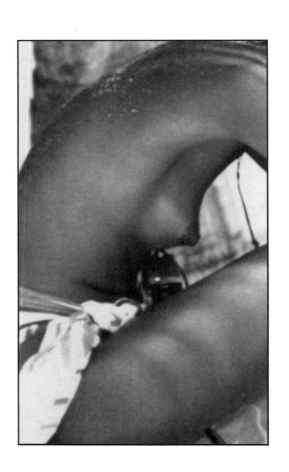

Jewelle Gomez

Piece of Time

E LLA KNEELED DOWN TO REACH BEHIND THE TOILET. Her pink cotton skirt pulled tight around her brown thighs. Her skin already glistened with sweat from the morning sun and her labour. She moved quickly through the hotel room sanitizing tropical mildew and banishing sand. Each morning our eyes met in the mirror just as she wiped down the tiles and I raised my arms in a last wake-up stretch. I always imagined that her gaze flickered over my body; enjoying my broad shoulders or catching a glance of my plum brown nipples as the African cloth I wrapped myself in dropped away to the floor. For a moment I imagined the pristine hardness of the bathroom tiles at my back and her damp skin pressed against mine.

"Okay, it's finished here," Ella said as she folded the cleaning rag and hung it under the sink. She turned around and, as always, seemed surprised that I was still watching her. Her eyes were light brown and didn't quite hide their smile, her hair was dark and pulled back, tied in a ribbon. It hung lightly on her neck the way that straightened hair does. My own was in short tight braids that brushed my shoulders; a coloured bead at the end of each. It was a trendy affectation I'd indulged in for my vacation. I smiled. She smiled back. On a trip filled with so much music, laughter and smiles, hers was the one that my eyes looked for each morning. She gathered the towels from the floor and in the same motion opened the hotel room door.

"Goodbye."

"See ya," I said, feeling about twelve years old instead of thirty. She shut the door softly behind her and I listened to the clicking of her silver bangle bracelets as she walked around the verandah toward the stairs. My room was the last one on the second level facing the beach. Her bangles brushed the painted wood railing as she went down, then through the tiny courtyard and into the front office.

I dropped my cloth to the floor and stepped into my bathing suit. I planned to swim for hours and lie in the sun reading and sip margueritas until I could do nothing but sleep and maybe dream of Ella.

One day turned into another. Each was closer to my return to work and the city. I did not miss the city nor did I dread returning. But here, it was as if time did not move. I could prolong any pleasure until I had my fill. The luxury of it was something from a fantasy in my childhood. The island was a tiny neighbourhood gone to the sea. The music of the language, the fresh smells and deep colours all enveloped me. I clung to the bosom of this place. All else disappeared.

In the morning, too early for her to begin work in the rooms, Ella passed below in the courtyard carrying a bag of laundry. She deposited the bundle in a bin, then returned. I called down to her, my voice whispering in the cool, private morning air. She looked up and I raised my cup of tea in invitation. As she turned in from the beach end of the courtyard I prepared another cup.

We stood together at the door, she more out than in. We talked about the fishing and the rainstorm of two days ago and how we'd spent Christmas.

Soon she said, "I'd better be getting to my rooms."

"I'm going to swim this morning," I said.

"Then I'll be coming in now, all right?"

"I'll do the linen," she said, and began to strip the bed. I went into the bathroom and turned on the shower.

When I stepped out the bed was fresh and the covers snapped firmly around the corners. The sand was swept from the floor tiles back outside and our tea cups put away. I knelt to rinse the tub.

"No, I can do that. I'll do it, please."

She came toward me, a look of alarm on her face. I laughed. She reached for the cleaning rag in my hand as I bent over the suds, then she laughed too. As I kneeled on the edge of the tub, my cloth came unwrapped and fell in. We both tried to retrieve it from the draining tub. My feet slid on the wet tile and I sat down on the floor with a thud.

"Are you hurt?" she said, holding my cloth in one hand, reaching out to me with the other. She looked only into my eyes. Her hand was soft and firm on my shoulder as she knelt down. I watched the line of the muscles in her forearm, then traced the soft inside with my hand. I pulled her down and pressed my mouth to hers. My tongue pushed between her teeth as fiercely as my hand on her skin was gentle.

Hers arms encircled my shoulders. We lay back on the tiles, her body atop mine, then she removed her cotton t-shirt. Her brown breasts were nestled insistently against me. I raised my leg between hers. The moistness that matted the hair there dampened my leg. Her body moved in a brisk and demanding rhythm.

I wondered quickly if the door was locked, then was sure it was. I heard Ella call my name for the first time. I stopped her with my lips. Her hips were searching, pushing toward their goal. Ella's mouth on mine was sweet and full with hungers of its own. Her right hand held the back of my neck and her left hand found its way between my thighs, brushing the hair and flesh softly at first, then playing over the outer edges. She found my clit and began moving back and forth. A gasp escaped my mouth and I opened my legs wider. Her middle finger slipped past the soft outer lips and entered me so gently at first I didn't feel it. Then she pushed inside and I felt the dams burst. I opened my mouth and tried to swallow my scream of pleasure. Ella's tongue filled me and sucked up my joy. We lay still for a moment, our breathing and the seagulls the only sounds. Then she pulled herself up.

"Miss..."she started.

I cut her off again, this time my fingers to her lips, "I think it's okay if you stop calling me Miss!"

"Carolyn," she said softly, then covered my mouth with hers again. We kissed for moments that wrapped around us, making time have no meaning. Then she rose. "It's getting late, you know," she said with a giggle. Then pulled away, her determination not yielding to my need. "I have my work, girl. Not tonight, I see my boyfriend on Wednesdays. I better go. I'll see you later."

And she was out the door. I lay still on the tile floor and listened to her bangles as she ran down the stairs.

Later on the beach my skin still tingled and the sun pushed my temperature higher. I stretched out on the deck chair with my eyes closed. I felt her mouth, her hands and the sun on me and came again.

Ella arrived each morning. There were only five left. She tapped lightly, then entered. I would look up from the small table where I'd prepared tea. She sat and we sipped slowly; then slipped into the bed. We made love, sometimes gently, other times with a roughness resembling the waves that crashed the seawall below.

We talked of her boyfriend, who was married and saw her only once or twice a week. She worked at two jobs, saving money to buy land, maybe on this island or her home island. We were the same age, and although my life semed to already contain the material things she was striving for, it was I who felt rootless and undirected.

We talked of our families, hers so dependent on her help, mine so estranged from me; of growing up, the path that led us to the same but different place. She loved this island. I did too. She could stay. I could not.

On the third morning of the five I said, "You could visit me, come to the city for a vacation or ...."

"And what I'm going to do there?"

I was angry but not sure at whom: at her for refusing to drop everything and take a chance; at myself for not accepting the sea that existed between us, or just at the blindness of the circumstance.

I felt narrow and self-indulgent in my desire for her. An ugly, black American, everything I'd always despised. Yet I wanted her. Somehow, somewhere it was right that we should be together.

On the last night after packing I sat up with a bottle of wine listening to the waves beneath my window and the tourist voices from the courtyard. Ella tapped at my door as I was thinking of going to bed. When I opened it she came in quickly and thrust an envelope and a small gift-wrapped box into my hand.

"Can't stay, you know. He waiting down there. I'll be back in the morning." Then she ran out and down the stairs before I could respond.

Early in the morning she entered with her key. I was awake but lying still. She was out of her clothes and beside me in a moment. Our lovemaking began abruptly but built slowly. We touched each part of our bodies, imprinting memories on our fingertips.

"I don't want to leave you," I whispered.

"You're not leaving me. My heart go with you, just I must stay here."

Then... "Maybe you'll write to me. Maybe you'll come back too."

I started to speak but she quieted me.

"Don't make promises now, girl. We make love."

Her hands on me and inside of me pushed the city away. My mouth eagerly drew in the flavours of her body. Under my touch the sounds she made were of ocean waves, rhythmic and wild. We slept for only a few moments before it was time for her to dress and go on with her chores.

"I'll come back to ride with you to the airport?" she said with a small question mark at the end.

"Yes," I said, pleased.

In the waiting room she talked lightly as we sat: stories of her mother and sisters; questions about mine. We never mentioned the city nor tomorrow morning.

When she kissed my cheek she whispered "sister-love" in my ear, so softly I wasn't sure I'd heard it until I looked in her eyes. I held her close for only a minute, wanting more, knowing this would be enough for the moment. I boarded the plane and time began to move again.

Ritz Chow

incantation

i will love you like wind,
intermittent and insistent,
unable to leave you
unmoved, hair or clothing.
i will race across your flesh
and leave no scar.
i will hover above you until
you scan the sky for me.
it's the search for the invisible
or the clues. you will know
            i am coming
when trees begin small trembles
at the tips of leaves,
when your scarf leaps
and dances towards the ocean.
there will be signs before i come.
i will arrive on your shoulder
from under a bird's wings,
hot from flight, burning with distance.

Ritz Chow

gros morne national park, newfoundland

the ocean blows its own cold body in small fragments onto our
faces and bare legs. the black volcanic rocks erupt into white
cloud above us — stoned heat, brittle with past. as we climb on
rocks amongst the tidal pools, we follow the white veins shot
through cliffs like trapped lightning. we stop for the rattle of
stones, not rocks. because stones are smooth. because stones
start so softly in the mouth then echo away. we look into tidal
pools with starfish in our eyes, but see only glistening shells
of mussels woven together: a live mosaic exposed. you take my
hand in yours, hold it tight because you can. here by the
atlantic ocean as seagulls web the sky with anticipation for
ebbing tides. here where your body ripples in its own trapped
pool, washed from ocean onto shore. here your eyes are the glazed
mosaic gaze of wet rocks; your hands, red lichen absorbing the
last drops of sun.

Judith Nicholson

Ebony Gem

what is this ebony gem
i have unearthed from this dark mound?

i will polish this jewel
smooth and round with my tongue
until it slips and glistens
and then tucks itself back gently
between the dark lids of your treasure mound.

Funny

how a woman can stay
in my mind like a song
her tune on my lips
all day long

me humming her rhythms
when i can't sing her tune aloud
with my mouth wide
and dripping with her wet verses.

C. Allyson Lee

Ki-Ai

EET KUNE DO CLASSES, MONDAY NIGHTS. According to the local advertisement. That was the martial art developed by Bruce Lee. I decided to drop in one night to check it out. I'd always loved Bruce Lee, watched all of his movies, pretended we were cousins. It helped that I was also a Lee, with short, black hair and a no-nonsense face. I'd plaster his posters everywhere. My white co-workers would ask: "Hey, are you related to Bruce Lee?" I'd reply, "I taught him all he knew." And they'd believe me.

When I arrived at the dojo wearing my judo-gi, I wasn't surprised to find that most of the twenty students were white men. I'd seen their kind before, the Bruce Lee wanna-bees. Flexing whatever they could, grunting and posing. Students and instructors alike, trying to impress everyone, especially the young women, with their ultra-macho antics. But I was not a young woman. I was an Asian lesbian in her late thirties, having already done some Tai Chi, Aikido and Judo in her earlier days. So, I wasn't going to be impressed easily.

There were only five women in the class, two Asian and three white. One of the Asian women looked my way and smiled, which prompted me to go up to her and ask questions about the dojo. I learned through her that this class had been going on for about a year, and that it was taught by two instructors, a man and a woman from Hong Kong. Good. At least there'd be authenticity.

I looked around the dojo. The air smelled of hard-earned sweat. Rubber mats covered the floor. Everyone was intent on stretching out. Not much talking.

Then suddenly, the sound of hands clapping together pierced the air, calling together all the students. The instructors came in, dressed in black mandarin-collar outfits, looking solemn and stern. No friendly hellos, only bowing. The students had lined up in front of them, kneeling down, silent. The man barked out some Cantonese phrases, and everyone jumped up. I was a third- generation Canadian born Chinese who didn't speak one word of Cantonese; I could only understand numbers and names for food items. I'd been used to hearing Japanese commands from other martial arts classes.

It wasn't easy trying to do the warm-ups, keeping up with everyone else. There were so many people in the room moving around, getting in the way. The man did all the talking.

I tried to sneak a peek at the woman instructor every now and then. She never showed one bit of strain in her face, no matter what kind of exercise she was doing. She was beautiful. About my height, five foot six, long, jet-black hair tied back in a ponytail. Strong eyebrows, striking intelligent eyes, no glasses. She looked about thirtyish, I thought.

The man began to demonstrate throws on her and I wondered how long she could keep this up while he grunted and showed off his prowess. Didn't she get to demonstrate on him? Apparently not, because he clapped his hands again, which sent everyone scrambling into pairs trying to imitate what they had just seen.

I had the misfortune of being paired up with a cocky, young, blonde man who was most anxious to show me how this technique should be done. He urged me to run at him and smash him in the face. When I obliged him, I made a forceful contact with his jaw, which sent him reeling backwards onto the floor. The entire class stopped. No one was more startled than I. The poor guy, he couldn't even defend himself against this old lady, the newcomer in the class!

Several men ran up to the fallen would-be fighter, then suddenly the woman instructor appeared in front of me. Taking hold of my right hand, which had begun to burn, she asked me gently: "Are you hurt?" The young man got up, aided by two men, and still holding his face, said to me, "Hey, that was good. Real good." And he smiled.

How peculiar. That someone would ask me to deck him and then thank me for it later. I apologised profusely, then said to the woman, "No, I'm OK. I'm really sorry. I thought he'd be able to counteract that!"

She smiled warmly at me, then said: "Sometimes our guys get a little over-confident. But still, we need to exercise some control. I'm Hannah. And you're...?"

"Cassandra."

"Okay, Cassandra, let's work together on this one."

Her voice revealed a mixture of British and Hong Kong accents, which I found intriguing. I wanted to know more about her. Between throws and blows I asked her question after question and found out that she'd been here for about ten months teaching this, and that she'd been learning the art since she was about eight years old.

I watched her slice through the air like an angelfish gliding in water. She was full of grace and confidence. Her force was so powerful and quick that I thought I was in a martial arts movie. I was entranced.

Asking out a total stranger had never been easy for me to do, especially if she was gorgeous and friendly. And this wasn't exactly a lesbian setting. But being with her was so natural and effortless, so I asked boldly: "You know, I'd really like to talk with you some more about all of this. How'd you like to go to the noodle place down the street with me after class? Unless you have other plans...."

She hesitated for a fraction of a second. She looked uncomfortable with the invitation. After all, she probably got hit on regularly (in more ways than one) by dozens of adoring students.

"Oh, I'm sorry. I do have plans tonight. But maybe we can do that next week?"

Rats! But what did I expect on such short notice? Trying to hide my disappointment, I assured her that next week would be fine. Then I felt a tingle, knowing she'd just asked me to come back to next week's class and that we'd be getting together after that.

When class ended, the students seemed to relax, loosen up a lot. There was lots of chatter and kidding around, and she was surrounded by people wanting to get her attention. I watched her as she warmed up to them, as though the end of class signalled permission to smile. And that she did. Her smile was full and infectious, with perfect straight teeth and fleshy lips.

Later, in the locker room, she seemed engulfed by the other women, as conversation became more and more animated. I couldn't help but feel a little left out, being the new kid on the block, shy in a crowd. She introduced me to the others, and we exchanged superficial pleasantries while getting undressed.

I kept wishing that everyone else would disappear so that I could have her to myself. And as she removed her gi, somewhat ceremoniously, I was treated to something beyond my wildest dreams. I hadn't seen muscle definition like this on any other woman, let alone an Asian. Not since I'd watched the physique competition at the Gay Games a couple of years ago. Hannah was richly tanned, tight and solid. Admirable deltoids and the most respectable biceps. Cut, but not lumpy or overstated like so many narcissistic body builders. She didn't have those disgusting veins that lie on skin like spaghetti strings. She had just enough everywhere to show that she looked after herself with pride and respect.

I tried to take this all in without letting on to anyone that I was watching her that closely, and I kept wondering why the others weren't as mesmerised by her spectacular body as I was. Were they used to seeing her like that, week after week? Lucky women. Or maybe they were all straight and couldn't possibly appreciate this work of art as much as a lesbian could.

I changed my own clothes in slow motion as I imagined what it would be like to be alone with her in this locker room.

She's lying on top of me on a wooden bench so hard and cruel, but I don't care. Her magnificent body presses into mine, and her sinewy arms and legs wrap around my overheated body in a blanket of unbearable passion. My hands move up and down her powerful back, feeling the rippling muscles of energy, pulling at her smooth, taut skin right down to her round, sensuous butt. She clasps both my hands above my head and restrains them, gently but authoritatively, while she lowers her face onto mine. Her hair, shiny and untied, cascades down over her shoulders, teasing my face and neck with tickles and sweeps. Her mouth, wide open, joins mine and she becomes incendiary, igniting a fire deep within my entire being. I am convulsing with want. Hungry enough to swallow her up whole, bathing in a pool of rhythmic desire.

Our tongues have a life of their own, probing and slithering, caressing every curve and crevice of each other's face. Then, as if to come up for air, I pull down to her chocolate-brown nipples and take one of them into my mouth, my lips and tongue sucking her in and out, round and around, tasting her succulent flesh, feeling it come alive and hard, until she cries out loud. Crying out as though she can't stand the thought of having too much of a good thing.

I wrap my thighs around her hips and swing her onto her back. And I bury my face in her chest. My hands glide down to her steaming belly and I taste her salt, drawing throbbing circles around her belly-button, making her gasp for air. My fingertips start to tease the outside of her bush which by now is glistening with beads of sweat. Then I dive down into her treasure, finding it juicy and sweet, feeling it pulsate for more. I give her what she wants, fully and willingly. The tip of my tongue exploring her valley, feeling her walls contract as she squeezes her thighs desperately against my ears. Her hands grip my head and she pushes me down hard, as if she is afraid that I may stop.

And as she drives her jewel into my mouth, she screams. The loudest ki-ai I've ever heard in all my life, and her whole body shudders. I am suffocating in her pleasure. Then we lie together, wrapped up so tightly that nothing, not even air, can find space between us. We melt together in a cocoon of tranquillity.

"Cassandra... Cassandra?"

"...Huh?"

Jarred from my dream, I blushed furiously, having been caught entertaining impure thoughts about my new teacher. Once again I had become a slave to my over-active imagination.

She stood in front of me, fully dressed, smiling down at me. I had no idea how much time had lapsed. She took my hand and squeezed it. "See you next week?"

"Oh, right. See you next week!" Then she left with the others, closing the door behind her.

Salimah Kassim-Lakha

For Lipika, ten years later
and now that I am bolder....

Inches

It was when I first kissed your cheek
that I realized that your lips
were no more than   inches   away

and if I had dared
            to cross
                        over
                                    those   few   inches

my life, intertwined with yours,
would change   forever

without a lie
this is the way that I want you

inches apart

your response welcomes me

Naomi Guilbert

memory

wanting you
my breasts remember
whole Sundays in bed
thighs clenched and sweating
bodies pressing
into sweet smelling sheets
those days
the laundry would stay
unwashed
the phone remained unanswered
ears tuned instead
to that sudden intake of breath
as my fingers slid
inside you
that summer
our laughter rang out
like soft bells
our desire was a liquid blue-jade pool
spilling onto the floor

and when we finally got up
legs shaking   some hours later
we only made it half-way to the kitchen
before deciding we were too tired
to eat
i remember falling asleep
in each other's arms
and i remember waking
and starting up all over again
voices rising like a steady wind
Mrs. Campbell banging on the wall
behind our heads
shhhh i'd whisper giggling
gently pressing my cheek
to your lips
and we'd go on
but softer now
slender fingers brushing
the inside of your thighs
small sounds escaping
long past dawn

Natasha Singh

Musky Rose

Smell musky rose
off your skin...
want to open you
like a flower
peel back your layers gently
and pay homage
to your centre,
want to make a garland
out of your petals
to wear around my neck
and carry with me,
want to close you in
between the pages
of a book of poems;
press your shape
your colour
your essence
into lasting form,
want to open it up again
and take you out —
take you in,
want to smell musky rose
on my fingertips
on this page
between these lines
long into the night
and tomorrow....

Sea Goddess

From a sea of depth
and stormy waters
you emerged —
your hair tangled seaweed
plastered to brown skin
blowing freely
as you rose like a spray
of something salty
something sweet...
pulling me in
you held me close
as I helplessly
rode your wave
until I could taste only
the salt and sweetness
on my lips,
on my tongue,
inside of me
tell me sea goddess —
after I've drowned
will you lap triumphantly
against the shore
of my existence,
or will you sing
a sad song for me?

Patrice Leung

Hey, Kids, Don't Try This At Home

ER FACE FADED ONTO THE SCREEN AND THERE she was in extreme close-up with five hundred and sixty lines of Sony electronics traversing her exquisite features. She was, to say the least, exactly what I wanted. Desire Incarnate. A nom de plume to be sure but one oh so apropos.

Her soft, full, sensuous lips were moving, and as it was deemed sexually incorrect to be transfixed solely by such a beauteous image, I turned on. The sound.

"... such a strong woman that I was immediately attracted to her."

Hey, she's talking about me. Hah, hah, hah. Isn't that right, Desire? You talkin' 'bout me, ain't ya?

Yeah, right.

Wait a minute. Did you just look at me?

Naaaaaah!

The image widened to reveal the insipid male (redundant?) interviewer who was droning himself into the annals of American culture.

Honey, you may look gooooooooooooood but you sure look bored. If you want someone provocative you better come on a my house. Hah, hah. And stop looking in the camera! You're only encouraging me. Hah, hah, hah.

"Desire, you've played so many quote ballbusters unquote characters, don't..."

"Actually, I wouldn't describe them as `ballbusters'. They're just people standing up against unfair situations. If you consider fighting against poverty, rape, racism, ballbusting you might want to ask yourself why."

That was good. He's stunned. And that ain't no oxymoron. Wait a minute. Did I just make you smile? You know, ballsy femmes really do it to me. Wink, wink.

"Heh, heh. Careful, I have a thing for strong women."

"I bet."

"No, really, I mean don't you find that because you play such strong women, especially since you're an Oriental woman, that you intimidate most men?"

"So?"

Oooooo, baby, I want you.

"Well, what I mean is don't you find men are afraid to ask you out?"

I'm not afraid of you Desire. If you think you can handle me call me....

"I'm sorry, I lost my train of thought. What were you saying?"

If men only knew that we don't hang on to their every word. Women can be so distracting.

"I asked you if you felt your personal life had suffered because of your professional choices."

Hmmmmm. I do like your smile. Warm with just a hint of irony.

"No, not at all."

Don't look at me like that unless you mean it. You better put your honey where your mouth is. Or better yet. Let me.

"Isn't it time for a commercial?"

"Uh, uh, I suppose. Heh, heh. You're the first guest who's ever *wanted* to go to a commercial."

Am I gonna be your first woman?

"I guess there's a first time for everything...."

I like that.

"Right then. Stay tuned folks. We'll be back in a minute."

The fading applause segued into an overly loud commercial. Muting seemed the appropriate choice.

Jesus, do I need to get back to work. Freelancing is a dangerous profession. Maybe I need a hobby between jobs. This t.v. thing can really fuck with your mind.

Ring, ring. Ring, ring. Ring, ring.

"Hello."

"Zoey?"

Jesus! Reality check:

"Desire?"

"What do you want from me?"

"Don't worry, I won't shoot a president. I just wanted you to know there's a world of women out here."

"Why me?"

"I'm not usually bowled over by other Asian women."

"Star fucker, huh?"

"It's a fantasy."

"Why you?"

"You deserve the very best."

"I've got to go."

"Just say yes."

"Bye."

"See ya."

I unmuted. The prosaic visage of the interviewer reappeared on the screen and banalities spewed forth from his mouth.

"Welcome back. We're talking to Desire Incarnate, the first Oriental woman ever to be nominated for Best Supporting Actress. Now Desire, are you Japanese or Chinese?"

"I'm more complex than that. Where should I start?"

Just relax. I'll start. We're alone in a room. It's a warm summer's eve, no not the one with vinegar and water, and there's a breeze gently wafting the curtains. You're standing naked by the window. I'm behind you. Close enough to feel your heat. But not touching you. Can you feel me?

"You're shivering Desire. Would you like the fans in the studio turned off?"

"I'm fine. Really. Please go on."

If you insist. I'd like to brush your hair back so I can see the beautiful line between your neck and shoulders. Hmmmmm. So sexy. I love this place on a woman. That's it. Don't be shy. Lean against me. God, it feels good to hold you. You feel so soft and warm. Can I nuzzle your neck? Can I kiss your shoulder?

"Please."

"Heh, heh. That's how you got the part, you just said `please'."

Your body's turning me on. I want to inhale you. I'm tracing the

line of your back with my tongue. Slowly. From the cheeks of your ass, up your spine, all the way to your neck, and behind your ear. Nibbling your lobe I can't resist darting my burning tongue into your ear.

"Desire, did you hear me?"

"I'm sorry."

Never apologize for making me wet. When you moaned it gave me such pleasure.

"Would you say you're ready for more challenging parts?"

"I would prefer things face to face."

"I beg your pardon."

No. I like you grinding your ass against my crotch. I like you feeling my excited nipples between your shoulder blades. If you lean your head back it'll be easier for me to spread your legs.

"Do you find love scenes hard?"

Yes you are. Can you feel my fingers spreading your lips and searching out your hardness? There it is. Maybe I should rub a little of your wetness on it. Around it. All around it. Like this. And maybe rub a little faster?

"Desire, is there something wrong with your chair?"

"Not at all. I've just been in one position for too long."

Kiss me then. Wait! First I want you to lick my finger. I want to taste you while you taste yourself. That's it. Suck it, baby. Now kiss me. Nice hot tongue you've got. You taste good, baby. I want more. Ah huh. No touching! For that you'll have to face the window again.

"What's next, Desire?"

"What's next?"

I want you to feel me touching your nipples. I'll flick each one gently until they become hard enough to squeeze and then squeezable enough to pinch. Hard. Yeah, that's it. I love holding breasts in my hands. Squeezing, rubbing, pulling. Just like kneading bread or squishing jello through my fingers. Let's force your nipples to fuck each other. Sssssssh! Such a noise!

"Well, thank you for coming. I must say it's been an interesting interview. I know you'll be even busier now but promise me you won't stay away too long."

How long has it been, baby? Hmmmm? How long since you let someone pay attention to that pretty pussy of yours? Or rather how long since you let someone who knows what you need pay attention to that pretty pussy of yours? Do you know what it feels like to have another woman's dripping cunt slide all over yours?

"It's been a pleasure."

"Good. I'm glad you enjoyed yourself."

"I promise I'll come again soon."

Give it to me, baby. Spread your legs and let me smell you. Ain't you a yummy girl? Your inner thighs are warming my lips. I want to kiss your stickiness. Can you feel the softness of my tongue in you? Open a little wider so I can look inside.

"Desire what are you doing? Uh, ladies and gentlemen..."

Don't look at me. It'll spoil the fun. Close your eyes and imagine me.

"Oh, my... Desire... you'll hurt yourself..."

CRASH!!

Whoa! Wait a minute! What are you doing in my living room?

"Turn off your television."

"You mean what's left of it."

"Turn it off."

"Okay. Okay. Satisfied?"

"Not yet. Now show me what you want."

I've really got to get a hobby.

"I'm waiting."

"Okay. Okay."

Stepping carefully over the shards of glass I moved toward her and tentatively placed my arms around her waist. She smiled and put her arms around my neck. I smiled back at her. And then she kissed my soul.

N. Sc. Woo

Kisses and Hugs
Luscious Licks and Rhythmic Strokes
Heavy Breathing and Sensual Pleasures
Creamy Delight and Mutual Ecstasy...

DO YOU FEEL ME
close to you
over you
under you
beside you
and inside you...

DO YOU?

Take me to the place where
ROSES
STAY
FOREVER
RED.

Naomi Guilbert

what i want

a princess to carry me off
into a different kind of sunset
laughter breaking like glass
on the pebbled shore
black hair blowing
in the wind
i want to gallop past all my other dreams
of wanting   old lovers that didn't
work out   i would like to ride hard
for eight days
look up from my thoughts
and see that sudden flash of understanding
in her eyes
i want to abandon my grief
along the side of the road
i want to be swept off my feet
and still be left
with a leg to stand on

Jenny Heasman

Fetish

I've never seen that before, you said, as you stared at me spraying
my pullover with deodorant.
It makes clothes smell fresher sometimes, I said.
I used to put scented soaps in my knicker drawer, you said.
What for? I asked. Who's going to know they smell of soap?
Well, you wear my knickers after I've worn them, you said.
That's because they're the first ones I pick up off the floor
sometimes, I lied, knowing I put them on after you because I like to
think of the smell of you against my skin, not soap-scented knickers.

Salimah Kassim-Lakha

a concurrent story of three lives

WHEN V. READS TO ME, THE DESIRE IS SMOOTH, like a ride in a little red Corvette.

K. says to me, "Salimah, I have something that I want you to look at...." My strongest wish is for her to show me her skin, the lines of her shoulders, to know that she can be stirred enough to contemplate desire and to offer that to me. Wish frantically for the contact, hoping to learn what she smells like. Think of her lips and wish again that I was more familiar with the texture, the pressure of how they might feel if she had held them for long enough on my skin. Hear her challenge, the one that keeps me on the outside, on the daily call sheet, but not in the intimate hollows of her mind or body. She fits nicely in my arms, I have felt her warmth and whisper in my ear. For K. I can hold out no longer, yet another woman startles my body with close contact.

she is a kiss on the wind

12:37 on a Tuesday night after many meetings and many conversations. I fold laundry in the damp basement of a stranger's house. I come across a pair of black socks that are not mine and yet are part of my possessions. I know then that I have been lazy, in leaving the laundry so long that I have to wash and wear items that are not really mine, and lazy in not knowing why more of her clothes are not part of my wardrobe — exchanged in the mornings that follow our evenings together. I think about the brown woman that these socks belong to and don't quite know where she is, or how she is surviving.

There are gaps in my own closet. Clothes that I miss, symbolically, because trust and continuity lapsed. And in wanting to reclaim these pieces, a part of me wants to deny that I ever made room to contemplate the impossibilities of sharing.

Travelling wildly forward in time to July 1993, to turning twenty-two. Do I look like the woman I imagined when I was twelve, or am I looking for that woman?

V. writes me into one of her stories. Her creativity tickles my mind. I think that in writing to each other we are megalomaniacs, that our versions of a situation, rather our projections, are the ones interesting enough to be scratched on the paper. Who seduced who? She's right, I think we might always argue about that. Who's to say whose ego is bigger, who most strongly wants to lay claim, especially after the story begs an ending.

Right now, we still argue about it.

As I look out across Toronto from her apartment window, the radiant lights from skyscrapers, almost fully lit on a Sunday night in October, compel me to speak. Now I look back at the woman of whom I have vague but excruciatingly precise images from the week that preceded this contact.

And within those thoughts I hear myself say, "This woman's beauty, in all her darkness, overshadows the city's most glamorous Saturday night display."

I quickly learn the nuances of her voice, a murmur in my ear, a deeply luxurious sound that presses on my centre of gravity. Of course I feel the tension of the unspoken permeate our conversation, yet feel easy enough to open my journal and, in a sense, let her consume a part of me that remains closed between black hard covers for most of the day.

Looking at her again, lifting my eyes off a white page I look into mahogany eyes that take me in and give me room enough to turn cartwheels.

Snap my fingers for time in my mind, knowing that earlier I had spent hours in the presence of blue/grey/green eyes when we were fucking, knowing that I didn't quite understand what passed through them and knowing slightly and then ever increasingly that she could never see into my eyes, let alone know the colour that they could be called.

Snap my fingers for time in my mind knowing that now I stand before beauty that belies experience, that offers acceptance in brownness. If I set a course again and follow it strictly, I see attraction and learn about loving the sameness, loving the colour that may have kept us from being here in this apartment at any other time.

I return to the present.

Pushing myself up against the wall of her bedroom, I struggle with words that could address the attraction. Hoping that she knows that I am at a loss because her beauty will finally destroy any appeals for light that might be found in me.

As rhythmically as my breathing I rise and fall from the opportunity to tell her I need to feel a response from her body. Willing her to read my mind or act on her own thoughts, I press my shoulders further into the wall and shake the lock from my knees. Her kiss in response searches for me, and the curiosity is brilliant.

Making a phone call home at 2:00 in the morning, I realize with a jolt that I had not planned on staying the night, but the thought of being able to spend a few more hours holding a woman of midnight colours close to me is all the invitation I need.

V.K. Aruna

Sutlej Cafe

> *(Author's note: This is an excerpt from a novella in progress called "Sutlej Cafe." Sumanthi is a South Asian lesbian born and raised in Malaysia who goes to the USA for a university education. While in college, she is accepted into a student exchange program to India — home to her mother's parents before they migrated to Malaysia. In India, Sumanthi experiences multiple displacements as well as returns to "homes" she never knew. One of her returns brings her in contact with Jodhi, a lesbian feminist activist in Pune (a city in central India, about 3 1/2 hours by train from Bombay). They don't fall in love immediately. But when they do, Sumanthi and Jodhi make up for lost time.*

SUMANTHI FACED JODHI... HER LONG LEAN silhouette against the semi-drawn curtains, revealing upturned breasts. Jodhi lit the oil lamps. A liquid glow gradually spread across the room. She placed the matches on the altar and turned her attention to several large square cushions piled against the wall. It was Jodhi who discovered that Sumanthi preferred the cold terrazzo tiles on the living room floor to the cotton mattresses in their bedrooms. The idea did not appeal to Jodhi, even on hot July afternoons when the air was thick with humidity. Yet the incentive was too great to ignore, so they devised an alternative — a makeshift ottoman of embroidered cushions that turned out to be a comfortable compromise.

Sumanthi helped Jodhi lay out the assortment of colours — sunset orange with red geometric patterns, parakeet green with brinjal trim, and a long black bolster with blue batik print on a sea of saffron wisps. Under the fiery glow of tiny brass lamps, the bed looked spectacular.

Before they first made love, Sumanthi had wondered if Jodhi would kiss the same as her American lovers, enjoy the sex games she liked to play. She had no idea how to please another South Asian woman.

A moist breath warmed the tip of Jodhi's earlobe, lips brushed the nape of her neck. Sumanthi kissed her softly, taking her lips fully in her mouth, pushing with her tongue till she was inside, then sucking urgently until Jodhi felt the twinges in her navel intensify like the flames burning in their pools of oil.

Jodhi breathed, quiet and measured. The delicate scent of sandalwood soap flowed from her skin, still damp from the long bath they had given each other a few minutes ago.

On the first night they met, Jodhi knew she wanted to sleep with Sumanthi. But something held her back. There was a sadness in the younger woman's eyes that made her seem withdrawn, almost guarded. Jodhi sensed that Sumanthi might want a friend without the complications of a post-party affair. She decided to postpone her intentions until she got better acquainted with the woman who kept insisting, as introductions were made, that she was "actually from Malaysia, currently studying in the U.S."

Jodhi filled her palms with the curves of Sumanthi's buttocks and kneaded the smooth flesh between long, hard fingers. This was the pleasure Sumanthi had never felt before with other partners... bangled wrists grazing her hips, hands that worked a printer's press unleashing new desires under her skin, smells of spice and oils that carried her back home. As the muscles in her inner thighs rippled, Sumanthi felt herself being lifted off the ground.

For a long moment, there were only sounds of Jodhi's bangles tinkling in symphony with the slow undulations of Sumanthi's body. Jodhi squeezed again and Sumanthi arched, her torso becoming a wave of fervid lava. Then, Sumanthi leaned over, seeking with her teeth the secret place on Jodhi's neck. She bit down, gently at first, then harder, leaving skin unbroken as the contours of Jodhi's broad shoulders shuddered and she whispered, "Again, do that again!"

A scooter beeped, a bicycle bell trilled, people rushed home for the weekend. For two years, they lived on separate continents, one in India, the other in America, and there had been no rush to find out what the other was like as a lover. Even when they managed to get to the Women's Decade Conference in Nairobi they spent all their time debating, flirting with their minds, pushing each other with philosophical discussions and heated political exchange. No one guessed they were already in love. No one knew they had been writing each other for months before coming to Nairobi. With time, Jodhi and Sumanthi understood how alike they were — fighters, loners, renegades within their own communities — the ones who served as bridges, opened channels, provided pathways — ones who were left hanging in the wind when the dust settled.

Two years after Nairobi, Sumanthi received a grant to work in Pune. Finally, they could live in the same house, eat the same meals, even lie in the same bed, this time as lovers, not only as best friends. Jodhi was ecstatic. She gave her sub-tenant notice and fixed up the room for Sumanthi. Her three closest friends helped her buy new window curtains, sun the mattress, paint the walls, hang a full-length mirror behind the door. They cooked up a banquet. Then chilled three bottles of champagne and packed into an old Ambassador to meet Sumanthi's flight in Bombay.

The soft folds of Jodhi's stomach quivered. Her breasts were already dancing in her partner's hands as their eyes met. She willed Sumanthi to pull and tug them, enjoying the way their words sparked unspoken between them. Sumanthi closed her teeth around a dark brown nipple, imagining a succulent Malaysian papaya, bursting with sweet juice. Jodhi pulled Sumanthi's head toward her other breast. Sumanthi bit down again. Rich nectar flowed down her chin as flesh melted in her hands. And the oil flames leapt in quiet unison along the window sill.

Pune was beautiful in winter — brilliant sunshine and crisp cold mornings that required a heavy cotton shawl. Nights became so chilly, the woollen blankets were pulled out from trunks sealed tight with naphthalene balls. It was a time to drink ginger tea to warm up one's insides, and to sip brandy, cocooned in well-travelled sleeping bags on the rooftop at twilight.

To the neighbours next door, taking in another quiet weekend evening, the women on the terrace seemed engaged in usual camaraderie, talking perhaps about work, movies, a newspaper report. They barely noticed the hand making its way discreetly under a shawl, fingers creeping quietly into a loosely-tied salvar, eyes locked in playful gaze. Yet, the neighbours knew the women stayed long after the sun vanished behind the hills. They knew there was something about the circle on Jodhi's terrace that was different. They even wished, sometimes, if they were women on those other rooftops, that they could join in too.

Sumanthi and Jodhi sank into the cushions, their bodies glistening as if they had just taken another bath. Jodhi felt Sumanthi's long thumbs glide towards the warm pulse growing stronger inside her. She let Sumanthi coax her thighs apart. Outside, sparrows twittered ceaselessly. A car horn indicated the neighbours were back from work.

For the first time, Sumanthi was with a woman who did not demand oral sex, did not make her feel deviant for being afraid of remembering the past. As the whirlpool around her fingers dragged her deeper in, she heard Jodhi groan at the back of her throat. Sumanthi freed her hands and slipped between Jodhi's thighs, feeling her nipples caress hair like wet velvet, like the fine moss that clung to hillsides after the monsoon rains. She rocked back and forth between Jodhi's thighs which grew tighter and harder around her until neither could move, only grind and sway in fierce embrace until the light that came through the window curtains changed to deep rose.

As they lay next to each other, their curled knees touching, Sumanthi said, "I'm getting hungry."

Jodhi turned and smiled, kissed the bridge of Sumanthi's nose, eyes travelling down the slack arms covered in fine brown hair, the prominent mound below the navel, the shaved long legs that ended in narrow feet. "We'll go out soon," she whispered and rolled Sumanthi on her back.

This time, a flame darted across Sumanthi's eyelids. It teased circles around her navel and reached between her legs. Jodhi moved slow and tender, each sweep of tongue like a serpent in search of food. Sumanthi writhed, fighting to keep her lover at bay, but Jodhi followed closely, not letting her get beyond reach. After a while, she sensed Sumanthi stay still, grow large and soft, opening to her touch. Jodhi immersed herself in the waters that flowed. Sumanthi moved up in rapid thrusts, her thighs fanning out to receive the mouth of the woman she loved, as pillows scattered, the street lights came on, and the television next door buffered the eruption of moans.

Kaushalya Bannerji

JOURNEYS

1.
LUGGAGE

Under the bridge I
Dreamed your skin   tongue   wet   thigh smile
Over and over

2.
EMBARKATION

Don't come to me like
A ship capsizing we might
Drown in love's water

3.
ARRIVAL

I dared my hand   there
Where your thighs part like rivers
Your desire, my sea.

Maxine Greaves

Shit!

The lights go off.
We're alone.
I feel your hand on my shoulder.
I reach out and touch your face.
You move closer.
Our tongues touch,
our hearts and souls touch.
Your body covers me
in a blanket of warmth.
Your body is moist with the
intensity of our passion,
my body is a desert,
it drinks up every bead of sweat.
Your mouth, boiled molasses
moving down,
my neck
my breasts
my stomach
shit... the phone rings.

Zahra Dhanani

Cunus Lingus or Chute Chat

It is
chute, yoni
cunus, clit
      cunt
any way you say
it still tastes
good on my tongue

It is
dy/ke/namics — hard
to figure out
hand/ling the tension
rolling it with
your fingertips, like
sucking on a raw onion
      submerged in
      juicy wet
layers upon layers   of lips
you are in ecstasy
but the sensation stings

It is
intimacy
In-to-me-see
is there more to know
than the
pulsating life
of my
yoni ripe
in between
your strong
brown
womon
hands, that
take me to a place
of yoni bumping and goldfish gobbling

It is
the locus of the lotus
the centre of the universe
POWER   STRENGTH
          CENTRE
It is here
where it lies
my mother's onion
the basis and root of everything

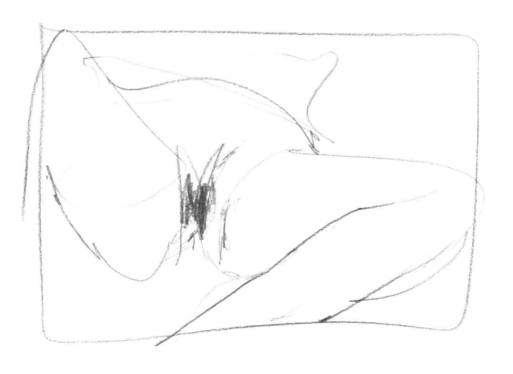

Nicola Harwood

shonna, last time

the familiar holds
a distant strangeness
invites memory to taste
the first sharp hip in
to belly

breath grasps the mouth
tongue still
hoping

hands over skin remember a turn
an opening
here

wed/wet with memory
the chamber walls harbour sense
artifacts
turned by hand smooth as stone enduring
I turn you
again and again

Carol Camper

Tea and Hattie

TEA PURPLE WAS A LESBIAN PROSTITUTE. That's "big L" Lesbian.... Tea was very proud and very out. Tea was an orphan. She never knew where her name came from, only that the sisters at the orphanage had said it was her real name. She kept this name because she liked it and just in case she really wasn't an orphan. She didn't want to offend some long lost rich relation. Her professional title was Tea Purple B.A. M.S.W, Wymyn's Sx Wyrkyr. The multitude of "Y"'s on her business card reflected her small "f" feminism. The fuschia shade was simply a match for her pussy. The card's small print by-line, "first times a specialty," reflected her talent for teaching and her commitment to the helping professions.

Tea loved to fuck and she genuinely liked her customers. With instincts like a mother cat, she knew who was "right" for her services. When vibes dictated against a particular liaison, Tea lovingly turned away her crestfallen customer with reassurances that the universe was indeed working to the good. No one resented this rejection, in fact Tea had a small fan club of women who would smile at her with bittersweet cow-eyed looks when they chanced to meet in bars. Sometimes the vibes would shift and the women would have their chance.

Tea did very well financially. Her rates were extremely varied depending on the customer's request, her ability to pay and Tea's mood. Tea was an excellent money manager. She invested wisely and her savings grew. Tea believed it important to regard one's clientele as investments and she carefully made sure that her customers were pleased with both her appearance and her surroundings. She had a lot of repeat business but even her most loyal clients knew that when Tea wanted new challenges they would temporarily lose their regular spots in her appointment book.

Tea had a natural and unique beauty but she also enjoyed the artifice of cosmetics and varied hairstyles. To describe Tea, her regular customers used words like "Amazon," "statuesque," "Rubenesque."

Newer acolytes just said "Wow!" Tea liked to eat hearty and healthy. Big was beautiful to Tea and she didn't want to lose in the size department. What would she do without those plump, powerful thighs to squeeze heads with? What fun could she have if her breasts were no longer big enough to smother with? Customers liked to cover her round belly with kisses and hang on like crazy to her big round bum. Tea took care of her chocolate skin with cocoa butter and washed her tight kinks with fragrant herbs and conditioned them with perfumed oils.

Tea set aside every Monday to do her major bodily care. It was her day — in fact she called it Myday, not Monday. This was the day when her robust, smiling masseuse (who was straight, dammit) would visit to give Tea the kind of expert attention she loved to give big women. The masseuse didn't want to accept pay for tending to Tea, but Tea insisted. She valued the woman's talent and didn't want to complicate things by taking favours which might lead to gratitude which might lead to fucking which might lead to losing a good masseuse.

Tea went to great lengths to please her customers. She always determined their needs through a phone interview process first. There were the tender young things who needed help on the way out. For these women Tea wore a particular type of outfit, a floaty, gauzy skirt which moved and swayed as she walked. She would top this with a loose fitting silk knit sweater. The neckline would plunge deeply, but Tea made sure that lacy camisoles filled in the "V" and slightly veiled her magnificent bosom so as not to immediately overpower (unless of course, that had been the request). Her body would be lightly perfumed and she made sure there were flowers and music, maybe Ella or Anita. She would start by offering a fragrant tisane and end with a breathless, grateful, shining eyed new customer.

Sometimes her customers were feminist therapists who would come to Tea because she understood. She did understand, because she had been one of them until she decided therapy took up too much fucking time. For the feminist therapists, she would wear her purple cotton pants, vintage Michigan Womyn's Music Festival tee-shirts and Birkenstocks — with socks. She would make sure there were beeswax candles all over, some good weed and maybe some Enya or Joni Mitchell on the CD player. The feminist therapists started out by talking for at least an hour and then they would throw themselves at Tea with passion and joyfully eat her like there was no tomorrow. Tea always enjoyed the suspense of waiting for them to initiate and they found it fulfilling that Tea had orgasms.

Some of Tea's favourites were the butches. They were Tea's most loyal customers. They treasured her professionalism and confidentiality. How many times had butches sought her out, stressed to the max from maintaining their studly reputations? In Tea's arms they could be topped by an expert, surrender for a while and no one would be the wiser. Even the stone butches would allow their lonely clits to respond to Tea's ministrations. Now when Tea topped, she never out-butched the butch, even though she was bigger than most of them. Tea was strictly a femme top and no one could doubt this, given the way she looked, poured into her leather capri pants, stiletto sandals and leather blouse. Yes, it really was a blouse. Tea had had it custom made and it featured a deep scoop neckline (all the better to show off cleavage galore) and it was accented by a six inch wide ruffle, yes a leather ruffle, and delicate stud-like snap closures down the back. Even the elbow length sleeves had huge circular ruffles. Tea used to wear a micro mini dress made of leather lace, thonging crocheted into lace until the butches said "For Chrissakes, Tea, can you make it leather OR lace? This is too fuckin' confusing!" But Tea could top with the best of them and the butches were mighty grateful. They paid better than anybody.

One day, Tea had to take her Himalayan cat, Sauerpuss (so named for her disdainful expression and love of pickled cabbage) to the veterinarian's. It seemed "Puss" had insisted on having a hairball even though it was Myday. Tea was not amused at interrupting Myday, but at least she didn't have to reschedule any customers. The masseuse had cancelled due to an emergency session with a feminist therapist anyway. Tea had just started thinking the masseuse was taking her for granted when Puss had started her ladylike retching. "Puss, if you would just settle down when I try to brush you, you little turdy, these hairballs wouldn't happen!" Tea exclaimed.

As she stepped out of her penthouse door, she noticed her new neighbour struggling with several bags of groceries and her keys. She had not met this neighbour yet. Tea put a protesting Puss down momentarily and went over to help the new neighbour.

"Excuse me, may I help you?" Tea inquired. A warm brown eye and a couple of grey dreads poked out from behind the bags.

"Thanks, Sweetie. Grab the top two bags, will you?" the woman responded with a warm, smoky voice. Tea took hold of the bags and her neighbour fit the key into the door and opened it.

"Come right through to the kitchen, Honey," the woman called, as she headed across the black and white tiled foyer. Tea noticed the African sculptures and bronzes which were on their crates, awaiting display. She noticed a pair of potted palms gracing a large arched doorway and a pink cattleya orchid blooming on a marble pedestal. She noticed that her neighbour was at least six feet tall, with an athlete's stride and a lush, African bottom. It was a bottom she could follow far beyond the kitchen. It was a familiar bottom.

The woman placed her groceries on the terra cotta tiled counter, plugged in an electric kettle and said "Can I offer you some tea? None of that herbal shit, though; just the best Ceylon Black." Tea started to reply when the woman finished puttering and turned around.

"Coach Johnson! I mean, Sister Johnson!" Tea sputtered. "My God, is that you?"

"Teap! Little Teap! Well now!" When Sister Johnson had been the basketball coach at the orphanage school, She had always used Tea's first name and initial and turned them into one word. Tea had never forgotten Coach Johnson, who was the youngest and the only Black nun at the orphanage. At thirteen, Tea had thought that twenty-five was kind of old (but young for a nun, she realized). That's how old Coach had been. She hadn't wanted to reveal her age but Tea and the other girls had dragged it out of her. Twenty years had passed. Lots of water had gone under the bridge and Little Teap, now Big Tea Purple, still remembered how her heart had pounded when Coach used to work up a sweat showing them court moves and showing off her fine self at the same time in those shorts of hers.

Now, Coach Johnson was leaning up against the kitchen counter, looking long, tall and plenty. "Call me Hattie" she said as she slid an appreciative gaze all over Tea's body. "Time has certainly made itself a gift to you, Darlin'."

Tea felt herself shiver. A whole flood of memories and imaginings overwhelmed her. At thirteen, she had not had a name for her feelings about Sister Johnson. She remembered the eagerness with which she had looked forward to gym class and the hours she and other devoted classmates had spent chattering and swooning over the vibrant young nun. Now, she knew that Little "Teap" (she suddenly cherished this pet name) had had an intense crush on the mysterious sister, this magnetic and handsome woman who now stood before her.

"Thank you" Tea said, struggling to regain her composure. "Time seems to have done a whole lot of good things for you, too. But you know, I really can't stay, I have to take my cat to the vet's but I would like to get together with you...."

"Tomorrow night, then," Hattie suggested, cutting into Tea's excuses. "We've got twenty years to catch up on, neighbour. Come by at seven o'clock. I'm cooking up some ribs and sweet corn."

Tea breathed her goodbyes and hurried back to collect Sauerpuss, who had wedged herself up against Hattie's door.

The next afternoon, Tea bid farewell to the last of her customers, a hefty Norwegian rower who reminded her of the masseuse. She headed for the jacuzzi, exchanging the Grieg CD for Lena Horne as she went. While the tub filled, Tea went to her dressing room and began selecting her ensemble for dinner with Hattie. Swooping a miffed Sauerpuss off the divan, she laid out first one outfit and then another. It was so hard to choose. Really, what does one wear when dining with a former nun? Tea gazed first at the jade linen trouser suit and then decided on the midnight blue silk pajamas. They were casual, beautifully cut and exquisite. She would certainly wear them to host a dinner, surely they were appropriate for being a guest as well, especially since her hostess only lived across the hall. Surely they were not inappropriate and boudoir-like. Deep blue was a dignified colour, even some nuns wore it. The burgundy charmeuse teddy for underneath, matching satin mules, and sapphires of modest size at her ears completed the ensemble. Tea went to the jacuzzi, set the timer for twenty-five minutes and stepped into the perfumed waters.

One hour later, Tea was ringing Hattie's doorbell.

"Come on in!" she heard Hattie yell. Tea entered to find Hattie bending over to check the pan of ribs, her bottom up in the air, presenting an arresting view.

"Smells good! I made some sangria. I thought it would taste nice with the ribs 'n' all." Tea set the large pottery jug down on the counter top. Hattie grinned up at her and said "Sounds good, Darlin'." There was a pot of boiling water into which Hattie plunged a half dozen cobs of sweet corn. She was wearing a pair of tailored black trousers, a sleeveless black silk shirt and a huge apron. Tea noticed that Hattie's long arms were still well muscled and that the cut of her trousers displayed how fine-looking her thighs were. Hattie was barefoot and she wore no jewelry.

They sat at the table. Hattie poured sangria and removed her apron. The corn was ready and the butter was handy, so they ate for a while in silence. Next, Hattie brought out a simple green salad and a loaf of corn bread. Tea poured more sangria.

"So why did you stop being a nun?" Tea inquired. The question was too obvious not to be asked.

"Oh, there was a bunch of things," Hattie said. "My Daddy died, and I was mad at God. My Mama died when I was little and Daddy was all I had left. He willed me his accounting business and in my religious order, I was expected to turn it over to the church. I knew Daddy wouldn't have wanted that. He worked with Mama for years to build up that business and so I decided to leave the convent and run it myself. I hadn't been happy in there for a few years anyway. I got to know myself better and it seemed like there were too many women and not enough women at the same time — if you know what I mean."

"I'm not sure what you're getting at" Tea said quietly, not wanting to betray her shock at Hattie's implication.

"Oh I think you know," Hattie said as she got up and went to the oven for the ribs. These she portioned out onto their plates and then she nestled a fat baked sweet potato beside each rack of ribs. They began the next course.

"I'm really not sure what you were implying before," Tea said again, wondering what had become of her usual brash self. She recognized the old, shy excitement growing.

"Girl, I've seen the streams of women that go through your door, even though I've only been here two weeks. I figured you must have been having some kind of good time in there and I was wondering when you would come up for air!" Hattie laughed while Tea's cheeks burned. Tea wondered if Hattie realized that the women were mostly paying guests, so to speak. She thought it might matter to Hattie. She hoped it wouldn't because that would be a shame. Tea liked her life.

"Hey, I'd never stop a woman from running a good business," Hattie said. "Are you enjoying those ribs? It's my Mama's recipe."

"Mm-Hmm," Tea nodded, "these are so good!" Tea finished the last rib and reached towards her napkin but Hattie grabbed her hand. She pulled Tea's fingers toward her mouth and started sucking the juice off.

"Mmm, this is the best part," Hattie murmured. Tea sat still, unable to move. Hattie took long slow strokes with her tongue. Tea liked it especially when Hattie reached all the way down between her fingers. When Hattie took the heel of Tea's right hand and bit down with her strong white teeth, Tea was wet through and through.

Hattie chewed her way up along Tea's arm, and by the time she got to Tea's shoulder, Tea knew she was definitely overdressed. She reached down to unbutton her top, but Hattie stopped her.

"Come with me" Hattie said, her lips pressed against Tea's ear. She led Tea down the corridor to her bedroom.

"Let me help you out of your things," Hattie whispered, removing Tea's pajama top. Tea's nipples were hard, and they were making themselves evident through the thin silk of her camisole. Hattie sucked them through the fabric. Wet silk always drove Tea crazy. She was about to kick off her mules when Hattie stopped her.

"Let me," Hattie said. Tea sat there, as if in a trance, while Hattie undressed her. Hattie slid the pajama top off and slipped the spaghetti straps of Tea's camisole over her shoulders. She knelt down in front of Tea and exposed Tea's right breast without touching it. She looked up at Tea and said "Kiss me." Tea leaned forward and their lips and tongues meshed. Hattie kept murmuring "Mmm... mmm." Tea's right nipple was still real hard, waiting for its share of attention. Hattie, still kneeling, pushed herself between Tea's thighs and wrapped her strong arms around Tea's back. She put her face into Tea's bosom, inhaling the sandalwood and began to suck. Tea's breasts were ripe and full and Hattie could take both nipples into her mouth at once. Tea wrapped her legs around Hattie's back and held on.

"Let me," breathed Hattie as she momentarily disentangled herself from Tea's flesh. Hattie peeled off both the camisole and the pajama bottoms. "The slippers are cute, leave them on." Tea was naked except for sapphires and satin mules.

"You're just gorgeous," Hattie said, looking up at Tea with dark, lustrous eyes. Hattie ran both hands up the back of Tea's legs all the way to her bum. Massaging there, Hattie put her face to Tea's thighs and sniffed between them. "Mmm..." said Hattie as Tea gripped her strong shoulders. Tea's legs were trembling as Hattie reached between them and caressed Tea's bum again. Then Hattie said "Let me" and pressed Tea to her face and slid her tongue deep into Tea's flesh. Tea moaned and sighed.

It seemed to Tea like Hattie's tongue had intuition. She had a subtlety and skill Tea had only believed she herself possessed. What's more, Hattie voiced her appreciation, crooning and sighing.

Hattie kept on licking Tea. She reached down between her own legs and played with herself. Her pussy was slick and wet, almost as wet as Tea's. Hattie kept on licking Tea. She moved her hand along the crack of Tea's bum stopping long enough to say, "Let me," slipping two fingers inside of Tea. Two fingers became three, then four and Tea kept on saying, "Yes."

Tea had her hands wound into Hattie's locks and gripping her tighter and tighter as her orgasm crashed. Wave after wave rolled out from Tea's pussy until she finally buckled, falling back onto the bed, pulling Hattie on top of her. Hattie held on tight to Tea, slipped a thigh between hers and began to grind her pussy rhythmically on Tea's hip. Hattie's breasts caressed Tea's face and Tea snuggled into their velvety softness, catching first one and then the other nipple to suck. Hattie kept riding, nudging Tea into another orgasm while she created her own. Fastened on to each other tight, tight, they slipped into the moment crying out and holding on for life. Tea and Hattie spent the whole night in each other's arms.

Tea went home in the morning and made ready for her first client, a feminist therapist; she noticed Tea's tiredness and inquired as to whether Tea was 'OK.'

"More than OK!" said Tea as she switched on the Loreena McKennitt CD and served up the camomile tea.

Tea and Hattie were lovers for a long time. They never moved in together. Across the hall was just perfect. Sometimes Hattie would give accounting services to Tea. Many times Tea would cook for Hattie.

Jenny Heasman

It's Not All About Orgasm

YOU MAY WISH TO ADJUST THE POSITION IN which you're sitting or lying. This is a story that has been asked for. Requested. A fiction I ask to be considered non-fiction. As a fiction you may read it as fantasy, but you shouldn't dismiss the possible. Relax and let your imagination go.

I imagine this as we're lying in bed together.

Naked we lean into each other, kiss slowly, lingering, feeling softness, rush of anticipation, savouring the luxury of time. Long, long, long. Licking your lips with my tongue, I wonder if you imagine I'm licking your other wetness. I feel your tongue in my mouth, circling — am I imagining your tongue circling my other wetness? Your hands exploring my body, mine yours. Feeling each other, enjoying touch we give. You can kiss me slowly all over my body, as I reach out to hold you. You can feel me move to your stroking and caressing. You turn me on. I know that realisation turns you on too. Listen to me. I want to hear you groan, feel you move between my fingers, feel you push your wetness up to my tongue and meet its rhythm. But it's your wetness on my leg that's happening. I touch my leg, I imagine your clitoris. You run your tongue gently over my clitoris and it feels like you take delight in covering your face. I want to feel your pouring wetness too. Imagine my turning you on so much you are as wet or more. I love going down on you, taste and smell mixed with the sound of your moaning. You pull me up so our lips meet. Imagine our other lips touching. They could. Lie back and think about our wetness mixing, swollen clitoris on swollen clitoris. Are you having to change position yet? You reach behind me and touch the source of my wetness, your hand moving up and down, sliding from clitoris to vagina. Some time I hope I can do this too. Kiss you from the neck to back, hands pressing the wall for support as I run one hand along your body, the other between your legs. Exchange them both for tongue.

Cheryl Clarke

interlude

late drinks
late talk
and a perfectly timed split
opening against
sheer blue-sheathed calf
denim desire
rough tight
ass against crotch
seamhard.
oh, clothes and the clothes you cover
till skin
till hands vanilla as can be
motion toward all zippers
among the xerographic
and foolscap
untutored   groping light switch
and moving consensually
to undo frontal closures,
proud to be easy.

Larissa Lai

tell: longing and belonging

tell you say your usual way
of getting information
I want to say
      I have a crush
      on you feel too shy
blush and say
nothing
or *I was thinking about*
      the way cars look
      on the Georgia Viaduct at sunset
      all that exhaust
      filling the air

tell you say but I
don't hear
go on thinking about what
your skin might feel like
on a heavy summer evening

tell you say
as the night turns into
the sound of English Bay
the wind crushing the shore
the wind in the sky
Stanley Park
splinter thought: bashers
(too lazy to lurk
in the windy dark)   *tell*

your voice above the voice
of the wind telling the trees to hide us
your arm slips around mine
the wind nudges the leather smell
of your jacket into my mouth
full of quiet
not sure what to say
       my heart going off
       on its own *tell* you say
but you tell me whose hand
made the first motion downward
to interlock with the fingers
of yours or mine
who turned first   whose
lips   tongues   teeth
met in the wind
moist and hot against the cold
smell of leather   vague girl smell
coming up through the skin
behind your ear where my nose
teeth somehow are
       hungry   pulling at the warm sweet layer
of vapour
that surrounds you   the way
clouds follow the celestial
Kuan Yin   pulling you in
       like a whole school of fish

hundreds of miles away
leaving you on the coast   whole
mountain ranges between us
I am left only with
the blips of memory
                              body flashes
I tell you in letters
        the way desire
                gushes up unexpectedly
      in the middle
of cooking rice   talking
or riding down the mountain
on my bike late at night
slightly frightened of what might be
there in the dark
        strange animals
            sorrow or longing

hot flashes of wanting
to feel your tongue in my mouth
or at my breast
coaxing a nipple
into speaking   the even pressure
of your hand
finding its way past my rib cage
        my belly a soft field
                        waiting   warm earth
inside
        the red earth   mortal
remembering blood   the way
            it rushes to fill   the most desperate
places

longing and belonging
heart wandering about
hoping for a place to pitch things
the material elements of my soul
        bed books couch cooking utensils
        computer paper pens...
                        longing for a familiar
set of walls   animals that might
want to stay for a while
as companions   strays
                    like me   wet
in the rain and
thirsty in summer   animals
or something
like love   or whatever
might keep still   if only for a moment
keep my soul from rushing off
                        somewhere else
looking for its ancestral village
longing for home
aching for a place to touch-
        the temple of communication
our minds   lips
arms   shoulders   breasts   bellies
legs   cunts touching
flying together   along the low curve
        of warm earth
                right beneath us
                        wherever that is

Melo & Melit

Creating Spaces

THE WOMAN LAY READING. SHE ENJOYED THE early mornings. It was her `alone' time. It had become a ritual, seemed as if she had done this for ages. She lay reading, masturbating, watching the early risers on the street through her window.

Her lover lay sleeping next to her. She had no objections to the `alone' time. "Go ahead and wake up at 5 am, I won't bother you." An ongoing argument between them. If one lover is a night person and the other a morning person, when do you fuck?

She rose and went into the bathroom. Bathed, returned to sit beside her lover on the bed and creamed her body. She lay back against her lover and continued massaging the cream on her legs and thighs.

"Mmmm...." She turned to look at her lover, who was smiling broadly, yet still asleep. She laughed out loud. "Must be quite some dream," she muttered amusedly to herself.

"Mmmm...." Her lover turned and the smile broadened on her face as her hips began gyrating against the bed. "It'll start soon," she continued muttering and nodding her head as she turned to the mirror. She reached for a dress hanging on the back of the door and slipped it over her head. It settled gently against her nakedness. "Too hot for panties" she reassured herself.

She stood in front of the mirror accessorizing and admiring herself. Again she laughed out loud and shook her head in disbelief as she watched her lover's sleeping reflection in the mirror. She grabbed her scarf, and draping it over her shoulder she reached for a long, light jacket from the closet. She turned and walked towards the bed, amazed at how sexily active her lover could be in her sleep. Reaching down she kissed her lover lightly on the lips. "Have fun" she whispered as she straightened up....

"Mmmm...." Her eyes closed tightly she enjoys the kiss. Holding on the slowly moving tongue she breathes deeply. First the top lip. Gently. Sucking, biting lightly, paying attention to it. Moving on to the bottom lip.

Special attention must be paid to draw it slowly. Getting it to pouty fullness. "Mmmm...." She presses hard against her mouth, teeth knocking, tongue invading her precious mouth.

Suddenly the mouth is pulling away from her. "No more please." Her lover laughs. "Get up, it's late. We're having dinner with my cousin. You know, the one I've always wanted you to meet. She used to be a lesbian."

"So what happened?"

"Not sure. Maybe we should ask her about it."

"What time are we meeting her?"

"Seven."

She reaches for her, pulling her back on the bed. "We've got ten minutes at least." They wrestled as her lover tried to get up.

"You're messing up my clothes."

"So stop fighting." She pushed her lover against the headboard and eased herself down. The length of her body covering her lover's, her mouth attentive to the space behind her lover's ear. Slowly lifting the dress away from her lover's body, she buried her head down under.

The three women sit close together around a small round table. A dish of antipasto, a bottle of wine and a loaf of bread fight for space on the table with an imaginative bouquet of wild flowers. They take turns telling stories, revealing themselves, the wine loosening their tongues.

"It took me a long time to feel legitimate as an artist."

"I know what you mean. There's this constant pressure, this ongoing questioning about authentic voice. Then the criticism...."

"Tell me about it."

"Too personal, not universal.... You get it from all sides. As if there is only one story...."

"One black story, one lesbian...."

"And somehow this one story has to be true for everyone... all Blacks, mothers, lesbians, artists...."

"But it beats nine to five" the cousin interjected. All three women laughed.

"I've done so much in my life, different careers, and yet I've always run from what I wanted most.... almost afraid to try."

"Is this about the lesbian thing?" asks one of the lovers. The other lover looked at her in amusement. "Always so bold...."

The cousin interrupted. "I like the boldness."

She motioned to the waiter to bring another bottle. It was getting late but they did not pay attention to time. The cousin continued talking as if there had been no lull in the conversation.

"It was so big...." The lovers looked at each other and laughed out loud.

"What was so big?"

"No I mean the love or whatever it was, maybe more lust.... So much going on, I just couldn't do it. It took too much out of me."

"But that's what I like about what we have," one of the lovers said. "It's all that, it challenges me and frightens me...."

"Well I think... I don't know. I'm not sure what I ran from...."

One of the lovers reached for a seasoned mushroom. Taking a bite she reaches over and offers some to her lover. "Mmmm... taste this." She reaches over to the cousin and gives her what's left. "Isn't it wonderful? Reminds me of good sex...." They laugh out loud again, gaining the attention of the staff and a few late diners left in the restaurant.

The conversation turned to food and they continue trying the different dishes, feeding each other, tasting. They stayed until the owner, too tired to make a fuss, ushered them through the door. A bottle of complimentary wine was offered in thanks for the large bill.

Soon they laid across the couch, on pillows. Shoes off, clothing loosened, they continued talking and sipping the wine, listening to soft romantic reggae they often played during these mellow, intimate hang-outs.

They had exchanged looks earlier. They had been together long enough to know each other's attractions. They would follow each other's lead. The feeling of intimacy is electric and all three women respond in their individual way.

"Come closer," one of the women said. The others, more comfortable with lingering hands, long looks and stolen squeezes, remain silent. The bold one speaks up.

"I think we should fuck. I mean we all want to — let's not pretend."

"There is something to be said for foreplay, honey. Innuendoes, touch, all go a long way in saying what you just blurted out so..."

"Shhh... It's all the same... come here." They laugh nervously.

"I guess there is something to be said for anticipation."

The women lean into each other, whispering. Sometimes a nervous laugh escaped as they became more familiar with the new routine. One woman stayed near her ear, talking softly, murmuring words not always understandable. The other lover used hands and lips to explore each breast, to gasp as nipples become erect.

Hands roamed and lingered over the expanse of the body and back again, becoming bolder as the cousin gave in to the waves of unexplainable emotion. "So long... Too long."

Suddenly time was suspended and for a long time the women were a mass of arms and legs and tears and profound emotion. The bodies intermingled in ways never before tried and their mouths lingered above thighs and hips and ass and at long last that place where they wanted to rest. With each stroke, each wave, they whispered and the lovers found each other there in that new place. Their lips met against the softly rough hairs which generously covered the cousin. Their hands continued their playful exploration and as they looked into each other's eyes they reached down to taste the juices which flowed onto their hands.

The cousin lay back wanting to move, to talk back, feeling herself climbing. "Too soon. Noo..." she screamed, fighting to hold on, wanting to pull the lovers into her, to consume them. She opened wider, wanting no barriers. Mouths, hands and voices surrounded her. She wanted to be active. To touch and taste and scream and laugh with raw pleasure. Reaching she held onto a breast, beginning to climb again, wanting to make it last longer. "It's only the beginning," one of the lovers whispered into her. "You can let go."

It was as if her body was being thawed and she felt a melting in her groin. Her movements speeded up and for one perfect moment there was no time. She arched her back and screamed out in release.

And the beauty that their bodies created, in their many shapes and various colours, rendered their plateau perfect for the moment. Then they were falling and there were screams of delight as they shouted out this new joy they had found....

A door slams, she awakens to her lover's voice calling. She sits up slowly, rubbing her eyes. Her lover calls out to her again. Her voice excited. "Honey, are you still sleeping, come on wake up."

She rises laughing. "Goddess, what a dream. She grabbed her bathrobe, walks out into the living room saying, "I just had the wildest..."

"Honey, hey look who I brought home, this is my favourite cousin."

She begins to laugh, extending her hand in welcome.

Kalyani Pandya

Sugar Bay and other stories
(After Ven Begamudre's The Evil Eye)

this is what happens when
i venture onto it the soft
mud banks give and the heat
surrounds my ankles i curl
my toes   clutch the wet earth
delicious   with each step
it rises to hold me   now
at my knees   now my waist
and soon even my face   green
secrets shift unintelligibly and
when the surface splits
everywhere there is: sky

Chrystos

You Know I Like To Be

bossed around in the sack but honey don't you be tellin me
what to do anywhere else cause you see I need to run my
own time & if I want to talk & talk & talk for 3 hours on
the phone with my best girlfriend you know you'd better
find yourself something else to do   You do what you need
to be doing & I'll do the same   My pussy is yours when I
say you can have some   Otherwise she belongs to me & if
I want to give her a vacation or 2 with some other fine
woman, doesn't mean there's any less for you   You be vaca-
tioning your own self & I won't say a word   Possession is a
drug-related offence & it offends me when anyone wants to
put a dog collar on me, visible or invisible, cause I ain't no
bitch   I'm my own damn woman & I like all kinds of trouble   But no screaming matches, no stuff about how you
can't live without me because you know I ain't your lungs
I intend to redefine those 4-letter words, Miss Love & Miss
Fuck, with my own body   Let's see each other when it's
good & take a break when it's hard   You're not my woman
& I'm not yours except when I'm coming   Doesn't mean I
love your ass any less   Means I love you more than some
2-bit teenage romance, honey means I love you like a good
woman should

for Bo

Eve Harris

True Story

THIS IS A TRUE STORY, AND JUST LIKE NARDO RANKS', it has an Indian girl with long black hair and light brown skin. She was standing in the 14th Street subway station on the uptown side. I was on the downtown side, waiting for the train to Brooklyn, when I saw her. She was all the way at the north end, leaning against the grey bin, reading a magazine.

I had seen her before, a few months ago. I was outside a Western shop on Hudson Street, looking at a pair of cowboy boots, and all of a sudden a brilliant red glare flashed in the store window. I looked over my shoulder and saw her: a pretty, caramel-skinned girl in a red fur coat. She was staring at me, but I didn't let myself make any assumptions. When you are as tall as I am, everyone stares at you, usually to see if you're a transvestite. I hurried into the store.

She was dangerously sweet. And here she was again. How many times had I said, if I ever saw her again in my life, I wouldn't be so shy? So, before I could think, I crossed over to the other platform. Then, the uptown express train came. I ran fast, but the train was pulling out just as I reached the bottom step of the stairs. I cursed out loud.

"Missed your ride home?" said a soft, low voice. She was behind me, smiling.

She was a little girl, big-eyed and big-mouthed. Her hair was collected into a bun, and flecked with perspiration. In the vee before the coat clasped, I could see her naked, glistening skin. I stood gawking at her, trying to think of how to start.

"You coming home from a club?"

She nodded. It was now or never.

"Clit Club?"

"No," she said, laughing. "Is that where you were?" She eyed me scornfully.

I shook my head. "Where did you go?"

"Nell's."

Time to try again. "Do you know Boy?" Boy was a lesbian bartender there. "No," she said brightly. "I only know George and Greg."

I had run out of angles. I stood there feeling foolish, hands in my pockets. She looked away. As loose as her swing coat was, I could see the curve of her bosom. I wanted to undo the coat and see what she was wearing. It couldn't have been much, because her coat wasn't very long and her big, firm legs were in green fishnet stockings.

My train went by. We stood in the near empty station in silence. Finally she said, "Since you aren't one for conversation, would you like to read my magazine?"

I looked down. She was handing me a copy of *The Advocate*. I laughed.

"Overgrown as you are, and you don't know how to take care of business," she pouted.

"I know how to take care of business."

"Yeah?" She looked up, her large kohled eyes bright.

"Why don't you show me what I'm going to have to work with?" I said, and undid her coat. The first thing I noticed was the smell of *White Linen*. Then I saw she was wearing a low, square-necked green dress that revealed the straps of her lacy red bra. I pulled at the neckline. Her breasts were large and soft and the nipples chocolate dark. I put my hand over her crotch. Her thighs squeezed tightly together. She wasn't wearing any underwear and I could feel her mound.

"It's kind of bushy," she said, shyly.

"I'll manage," I said, leaning into her. I felt her breasts press against my abdomen. She parted my jacket and buried her face in my jersey. I ran my hands up and down her back, massaging her shoulders. I began to press her flesh harder and harder. "You must have an awful lot of tension," I said.

You can always tell how hard a girl can take it by how hard you can massage her shoulders, and she could take it real hard. It was making me excited. I pushed her away a little so I could slide my hands into her coat and touch her skin. She looked up at me bashfully. Bending down, I kissed her soft lips. She drew my tongue into her mouth, and I felt her suck on it. She reached up to me, standing on her toes.

"How is it you're so hungry, a pretty girl like you?" I asked, finally.

"It's a cruel world," she replied. She moved her hands down my front, up my jersey, and over my breasts. Her short, brown fingers began to tease my nipples. Then she tried to lift the jersey up.

"You're getting just a little bit wild," I said, pushing it down. She pouted again. Her lips were lusciously thick.

"Are you coming to Brooklyn, or do you have to go home to your lover?"

"You think I'd be like this if I had one?" she asked.

I nodded.

She laughed. "I haven't been with anyone in a year, which is why I am letting you pick me up. I've given up being good."

"Oh, you haven't," I said, and kissed her. "You're real good." And though I was on a tight budget, I knew I couldn't wait. I was going to have to take her somewhere where I could lay her down. Feeling a girl up in the subway station is fine, but this one needed more extensive treatment. My underwear was so moist it was becoming a thong. "We're taking a cab," I said.

We went outside and hailed a taxi. The cabdriver was Indian, and they had a roaring conversation in Hindi as I wiggled my fingers through her fishnets and into her wet hole. Her juices were as thick as honey. She reached up and moved closer to the partition and I slid deeper inside her. "Hanh, hanh," she said vigorously to the cabdriver. Finally, we arrived at her apartment. She reached into my pocket and paid the driver. I discreetly wiped my wet fingers on my jeans.

"You know how badly I wanted to suck them," I whispered in her ear.

We rushed up the stairs and into her studio. She didn't turn on the lights. I locked the door, sat on the bed, and she slowly undressed.

When she was naked, she came and sat on my lap. I stroked her breasts, and began to lick their tips quickly. She pushed a breast into my mouth. "Suck them," she whispered, her fingers in my dreads, massaging my head. I lay back and pulled her on top of me so her wet crotch was on my stomach. Her heavy breasts caressed my face. I slid my fingers back into her soft, yielding hole. She moaned. She was very, very wet.

"You better undress before I get your clothes dirty," she said, lifting up.

I squeezed her breasts. "Do you have a dildo?"

She jumped up off me. "Didn't you say I'm pretty?" she demanded. I nodded. "O.K., so you are in bed with a pretty girl, and she's naked and she has her legs open to you and all you can come up with is to shove a piece of plastic into her?" She shook her head in dismay.

I laughed. "You can't take anything else."

"Yes, I can," she said, breathily.

I shook my head and began to peel off my clothes.

"Yes, I can." She said again, yanking at my jersey. She seized my breasts and flicked her nipples with her thumbs. "You know you want to."

When I was naked, she pulled my left thigh over hers. Dangling her breasts just out of reach of my mouth, she pressed her pussy against mine and rubbed herself against me, her back arched. I could feel her lips crushed against mine, and I could tell she had a prominent clitoris. I imagined what her pussy looked like. But imagining wasn't good enough. I tossed her down.

She opened her thighs, stretching her legs out. Her mound was bisected by a wavy line. I peeled open her labia and her clitoris bulged like a jelly bean. She was wet, but my hand is big, so I asked if she had any KY. She shook her head impatiently and lifted her hips. I told myself to stop because her hole was too tight and she couldn't take it, but my fingers plunged into her, and I wiggled in my thumb. Her thick, soft, honeyed walls pushed against me. I forged deeper into her openness, and the walls receded. I curled my fingers into a fist. She pressed her thighs together and turned to her side.

"Is it too much?" I asked, my other hand reaching for myself.

In response, she turned onto her stomach with one leg raised up so I could move more deeply inside her. I pushed and pulled my hand inside her as she moved her ass back and forth. She mewled as I plunged until I hit her plug, and suddenly her canal was flooded. She raised onto all fours and I began to fist her more rapidly, jamming into her until she was so open that I could pull out completely and easily move back in. Her thick cream poured onto my hand, arm, all the way down to my elbow. Then, she screamed.

"Don't hurt me," she gasped.

I stopped. "Do you want me to pull out?"

She shook her head.

"You don't know how much you can take," I said, sitting back on my feet.

She looked over her shoulder at me. Huskily she said, "Make me come."

I reached around her waist to fondle her breasts. "Baby, I knew it would be too much for you." I kissed the small of her back.

But she rested her head on the pillow, raised her ass and purred. So I ran my tongue down her spine. My hand was still inside her and I knew it would hurt her if I pulled out now. It would be much easier on her if I did it as she came. I moved inside her. She made low, quick noises.

Encouraged, I sped up. Her pussy was getting hotter and her softness was pushing against my fist as I shoved into her. It felt so good as her pussy responded to me, her meat sucking me in and trying to eject me out. My arm ached but I couldn't stop. My own sex was tingling with desire. I squeezed my muscles and fisted her fast. She rocked and moaned, louder and louder, until she sprayed out come like warm oil, all over my hand and knees.

Quickly, I pulled out. I licked her salty sauce off my fingers.

She turned on her back and I lay over her. She ran her fingers lightly over my skin. We kissed slowly and lazily, until my pussy couldn't wait any longer.

"Come on, baby," I said, pulling her on top of me.

"Why should I?" she sulked. "You made me wait."

I was aghast. "When did I make you wait?" I began rubbing myself.

"You didn't see me on Hudson Street a couple of months ago?" she said, her eyes half-closed and her sweet, thick lower lip quivering. "You made me wait until now to take care of business."

"I'm sorry, baby," I said, over and over again, barely coherent. I was in agony. The sight of her hole so open to my fist made my pussy so greedy. "Please," I begged.

"Why don't you wait a few months?" she said.

I shifted around uncomfortably. My own hand was not enough.

"Didn't your mother ever tell you not to torture little girls?" she continued, kissing my abdomen.

I grabbed her by her hair.

She eyed me defiantly. "Say you'll never make me wait again."

"Never," I said, and shoved her head between my legs. She opened my pussy and ran her tongue over it lightly, too lightly to do anything but torture me. I pulled on her breasts hard. Then she laughed, and began to suck my pussy, first gently, then harder. She ran her tongue along the grooves between my folds until she reached the center, and then she firmly picked up my clitoris by the stem with her mouth. I came in waves. She opened my thighs further and shoved her breasts against my throbbing pussy.

Finally, I pulled her up onto me. Her small body was heavy and warm and soft. I pulled the covers over us.

"Don't forget," she said, sleepily. "Don't make me have to really punish you."

I laughed. "I won't forget, baby," I said. And you know, I never did.

Makeda Silvera

Dreaming

"COME WITH ME," SHE WHISPERED,
gently pulling me towards her.
"Let's take a walk, it's hot in here and the music is too loud."
I followed and she led me down to the coast. "Take your shoes off," she beckoned, "feel the sand between your toes, listen to the sea whisper, watch it bathe the sand."

I was spellbound by this woman, this almost-stranger who was so alluring. I walked beside her, quietly listening as she led me through her landscape, for this was her country and I was a visitor.

"Is this your first time on the island?" she asked. I nodded. "Well, it's not a very big place – you can get from one end of the island to the other in four hours.... I've lived here all my life."

For such a small place we seem to be walking a long time.

She pulled my hands into hers. "I want to show you a place." We headed towards some big white rocks. "Come, let's sit for a while," she said, motioning at the arch of a huge boulder. We sat in the dark, listening to the heavy waves.

"This is my favourite place, it's the roughest part of the island – the descent to the sea is steeper and the hills run closer to the coastline ... it's so wild ... so untamed ...."

She looked at me with what I thought was a challenge. How much did she really knew about me? She was in her late forties, with children. I knew nothing else about her.

"Tell me about yourself," she pursued.

"Well, there's not that much to tell. I'm a feminist, a sometime-musician, and I hold a part-time job in a women's book store to keep my travelling spirit alive."

"I gather you move around quite a bit," she mocked, then brushed a thick lock of hair away from my face. I could feel her body's heat close to mine as she began to stroke my neck with her forefinger.

"Yes," I said slowly, "but never to a place like this."

The surf is restless, for this place is where the Atlantic and the Caribbean Sea meet. Now our mouths out-sweeten the fresh warm sweet juice of sugar cane. Her hand slips under my white cotton shirt and my breast is waiting, her finger tips circle my breast, round and round, my nipples are brushfire. She is the wind come to send the fire through the valley. Her teeth along the contours of my breast make lightning flash against water, fire meet water. I feel danger and prophecy, and a scream slips out of my mouth and into the sea. My lover enters the mother of pearl, going home.

Waves splash blue/black in the moonlight creeping over the rock. The stars are a patchwork silver quilt. I ease her to the sand against the rocks, undress her slowly, taking care with each piece of clothing. Her black panties, I leave on.

"Kiss me there," she breathes, her body moving quick and bold against the sand. I kneel to kiss her full, round breast, in a manner that belies my passion. This is a public beach, not an exclusive tourist resort, but for someone who has lived on this island all her life my lover seems oblivious to the dangers. I forget too, swept up in her skin, her body soft and full, her legs firm and muscular. Her breasts have lost some tautness, yet offer a different sweetness. Her stomach is plump and soft to touch, like home-made jelly, and I play my tongue on it, trace the stretch marks. My fingers in her dark thick hair are in morning dew.

I run my hand against the dark hair on her legs, my finger opens her but gently, effortlessly, like a twig on water.

Without a whisper, without a sound, her hands command more fingers/move faster/go deeper into the river. Her breathing says she is about to break.

"Wait," I navigate. "Hold on, don't break the wave." I gently ease her bottom off the sand and tease my fingers into her ass to prolong the moment. She responds the way I want her to ... waiting ... begging.

My fingers enter the river once more. Her meeting rhythm demands. Wetness flows over fingers/hand/wrist. Her cries are nightbirds blending into the sea and taking off. I hold her tight, kiss her eyes, play my tongue again on her generous chocolate lips. Like driftwood, I float on the sea, its raw smell wills me to sample fish, suck salt.

"Sit on me, " she screams. "Ride me."

Her body feels good against mine. The sand sifts time between our legs. Once again she is about to scream into the ocean, but I pull back. Our bodies rub against sand, hips to hips, breasts to breasts, legs entwined, clothed only in a cool tropical breeze.

Sand to the touch of my tongue on body. She breaks and breaks again, holding on tight, legs twisting against legs, the ride is exuberant.

"I love you!" she shouts, so high on the ride.

"I love.... I love this night," I answer.

The wave of the sea covers our voices like a sheet. We are locked together, bound, sweet woman, witch, she-devil, goddess, bitch, whore, mother, sister, lover. We know nothing outside of us, nothing except each other by the rocks in the place where the ocean meets the sea. This time we both come. The night stretches like a blanket....

I am dreaming and I like it.

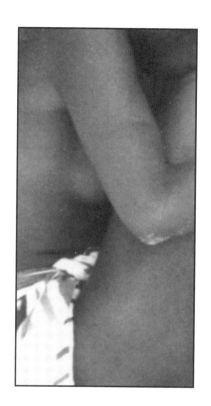

Little Earthquake

mother tongue
for zahra and anju

i sing of her without apology
how her mouth pursues openings
with revelations from suns
i tremble at the sight of her lips
engorged
spilling secrets of our woman
into hands waiting for red monsoons
the pleasure of tasting
the sudden brightness of ruby wings
mesmerizing intrusions of tongue
into blood running deeper than age

she is *kameshwari*
and there are so many words
in our mother's tongues
which have no translation
into new desire, unfulfilled:

chaahat maang shobha prem
aashiqi muhabbat rasabhava

we join our tongues
and invent a new language
though we have never been wordless
speaking of love

kameshwari   goddess of love
chaahat, maang   desire
shobha   beauty
prem   love
aashiqi   lover
muhabbat   passion
rasabhava   emotion

N. Sc. Woo

"GET ON YOUR BACK!"
In the warmth of our love
In the sweat of our passion
A tent of smoldering heat ready to explode
Straddling you
I lower myself
Opening and spreading my hood around your lovely lips
Feeling you beneath me
Sliding my fingers through your silky hair
Interlocking my fingers behind your neck
I draw you to me
Wanting you closer
Wanting you to suck my whole being into you
Coalescing
Can we get any closer?
I push myself onto you
Bucking like a wild horse, as only you can do to me,
I erupt and flood all over you
My love and lust
for you and only you
melts down your mouth, neck and shoulders...

Like a snow capped mountain peak glistening against the
velvety star speckled sky that has just experienced its first
snow fall?

Like the first cherry blossom amidst a forest of wavering
bamboo leaves that spreads its petals expounding the
wonders of spring?

Like a sundae with dark chocolate sauce blanketing the
virgin white soft cream?

Lisa Valencia-Svensson

Passion

My body is raging
With the fury of midsummer
Nights so cool they
       tingle and bless you
Days so hot they
       burn you alive

I feel the rain
Pouring down through my bones
Washing in me with a surge of sweetness
       My nights spent
       Sheets tossed aside

My tenderness breaks loose
My body giving in up out
To the madness and the longing
       I no longer hide

Cheryl Clarke

Living as a Lesbian at Forty-Five

Oh, it's a frequent dream:

He (He?) comes home hot and
wanting too.
You're in your room and wanting too
but wanting to control and orchestrate
so you can get it without really
acknowledging it will have a past
this
one way or another
in concert or in solitude
late
your juices built up from the day
odours sanguine
in the mood to take yourself
you set your works and toys out
and him
even though he knows you're a lesbian
there are those times
he still loses his crotch
in the part of your ass through your dress.

And that's how it happens
and it doesn't happen just once
and you may have work like poetry
to do like now and it starts
making you
pay it
some attention
and you run
and get your accoutrements
in excessive solitude
and space ephemeral with wetness.

Dear One

Why take so long to ask for it?
Come on, girl, are you gonna go after it?
Two days.
I'm only here for four.
Must you be courted so?
Your lovely breasts want
to linger over me.
It's pouring out of you.
I called you weeks ahead
so you could free yourself up.

You bragged that you'd risk the taste
of a stranger's juices,
so committed to desire's destination,
your mouth, the flow of menses.
But you won't take the first step with me.
I have to undress you, undress myself,
pull down the bedclothes,
push you between them,
get on top of you,
stretch the latex, and
talk you through it.

I been travelling to you for four years
from a desperate place
of grimy concrete and oxidized bronze.
I'm tired of assumptions.
Can't you just enter, kneel,
and make me first?
That's why I picked you.

C. Allyson Lee

Aishiteru

HELLO?

Hey there!

OH HI!

Did I wake you?

NO. I JUST GOT OUT OF THE SHOWER.

Mmmm. Then you're all squeaky clean! Did you put on the scented oil?

M-HMMM...

So, what are you wearing?

MY ROBE. THE BLACK SATIN ONE.

Hmmmm... is it open?

AAAH... PART WAY...

Are you lying on your bed?

UHH... LET ME JUST CLOSE THE DOOR... O.K.... NOW, WHERE WERE WE?

Are you holding the phone with your left hand?

YES.

What's your right hand doing?

RESTING ON MY CHEST.

Well, I want you to move it up to your face. Give your beautifully soft cheeks a light caress. Then move down along your throat and keep going down... run your fingers along that lovely collarbone and stroke that delicious middle part of your chest.
Hello... are you still there?

MMMMM...

Where's your hand now?

ON MY BREAST.

M...MM! Well, then, I want you to trace your fingers along the side of it. Feel the softness, the roundness. Make a circle around it... round and round. See how smooth your skin is. Now I want you to cup your whole hand onto your breast. Stroke that luscious nipple... gently... just to wake it up. Feel anything?

HMMM...

Now give that little maple bud a little squeeze between your fingers. Feel good?

AAAHHH...

Now bring your hand down the front. Loosen up that tie. Open that robe right up. Just glide your hand down. Right to your belly button. Touch that soft part around it. Feel that nice little dip. That little crater. I can feel my tongue on it now. Where's your hand now?

LOWER...

Where?

WHERE DO YOU THINK? ON MY HAIR...

Is it warm?

...VERY...

Then I want you to rest your whole hand over that fuzzy, dark mound. Let your fingers drape themselves down over... well, you know... hey! You're breathing kind of fast.

MMM... I'M ALL WET...

Where?

YOU KNOW WHERE!

All over your lips?

YES...

I don't believe you.

(gasp)...WHAT (distractedly)?...

I said, I don't believe you. You're going to have to prove it. You're going to have to go inside. Take that long, graceful finger and put it on top of that wet part. Are you ready to go in? Oh, but not just yet... just play with your fingertip over the opening. Tease it a bit. You like that? Are you opening up? Are you ready? Then just suck it right in. You know you want it. Are you in?

YES!

Well, you're not talking very much... having trouble breathing? Mmm? Are you moving around in that hot little cave of yours? Can I dive into your ocean?

OHHHH...

I want you to slide in and out, slowly. Feel it? Now bring all the wetness outside...

MMMMM...

Oh, you don't want to come out yet? Well, then, why don't you plunge back inside again? Go ahead... are you in again?

(gasp)

Well, I guess you're still having trouble talking. Got your mind on something else? Hmm?

I can hear you breathing faster and faster now. Now I want you to rub that beautiful little button of yours. Right now. All around it... that's it. But not too hard. Just a little bit... be good to yourself. You know you deserve it. You know you want it bad. And you want it good.

Feels so good, doesn't it? Up and down. Side to side. It's a full moon outside. All round and beautiful. Beautiful like you. You know, I'm lying right on top of you. My hand on yours, moving with you. On you, in you.

You just stay on that button. I want to slip inside you for a bit. Suck me right in. That's it... but, I think I'll come out now.

Don't worry. I just want to give you a good licking. Want to taste your juices. All that honey. I don't know if all this wet is coming from you or from me. I'm going to suck you dry. But is that possible? Your cup runneth over... there's plenty where that came from. You know, I don't think it's possible for you to be dry.

Go ahead, push onto my face... that's it. I want you to come all over my face. Squeeze me between your thighs... I'm holding you. Squeezing your cheeks, lifting you up so that I can take you in.

You're pulsating all over, throbbing. Squeezing. Hot. Dripping. Go ahead. Scream into the phone. Into me, Baby. Scream at the moon. Yeah, that's it. There...

So hot. So wet. Bathed in sweat. Both of us. Relax... lie back and enjoy it. You're breathing a little slower now... you O.K.?

(sigh) MMMMM...

I love you, Baby.

AISHITERU.
Aishiteru.

(knock, knock)

What was that?

HANG ON A MINUTE... I'LL SEE...

(pause)

THAT WAS MY MOTHER. SHE JUST GOT HOME.

But it's 2:00 in the morning! What did she want?

SHE WANTED TO KNOW IF I WANTED SOMETHING TO EAT.

Nicola Harwood

good times

yeah maybe the best time was in the truck on our way
to my sister's for supper already late I said
pull over
on that dark stretch of road between the golf course and the sea
I spread my legs you go down between my ass and the gear shift
or maybe it was the 1st of July
on Slocan Lake the fireworks across the water in New Denver
camping in the cold rain my shirt pulled up my breasts hollering
spraying milky electricity all over the wet beach
Garth and Jude's kitchen floor standing hips hard against
the cutlery drawer your hair in my fist
fucking
lips sucking
the new lavender dildo christmas morning wet as fish
net stockings, high heels and a black bra with silver studs
your hand up my bare ass the other hand grabbing that bra like reins
baby
maybe it was that time
yeah or maybe it's good and
that's all I need
to know

Billy E.

My Cha Cha Cha Baby

What shall we do? The Cha-Cha?
Yes, let's cha-cha baby!
Come here! Close to me!
The music starts, we look into one another's eyes,
I feel the pulse from our hands and torsos.
I start to lead her through the dance.
We move our bodies very well together, I notice!
Her black dress is flowing between my legs.

As I lead her back and forth, her legs come right between my legs, touching and rubbing me, feeling the material, feeling our bodies so close. The music plays Latin sounds, rhythm and drums. These sensations move through me, so full of excitement.

"I don't want to take my eyes off you," I say. "We must dance, only dance!"

"I want to feel you dancing with me tonight."

This dancing sensual delight tonight.

She stares into my eyes.

Her high heels and stockinged legs, come between my legs.

As I reach for her dress to lift, she looks intensely into my eyes.

I say to her, "I want you cha cha cha baby and we must dance, you are gonna like this dance, this is the way I do the Cha Cha Cha."

She smiles at me, I know she wants it too.

She is not resisting.

I continue to take her through the steps as I bring her close to me she feels my dildo.

Her eyes open up and she smiles once again.

She can feel my bulge.

I can feel her rub so slightly, as she kicks up one leg outside my leg. My cunt feels her heat.

I twirl her around. This time she comes back toward me before I lead her.

I say to her softly, "No! No!, I am the lead."

She steps back slightly to her place.

As I dance, I slide my hand up her leg further this time, I feel her soft bare ass and garter.

I am getting so wet.

We dance more and more.

Once again she comes toward me. "I am the lead," I say.

I bring her back once again, I turn her into a spin.

I bring her back to me to meet my special bulge.

She sways her legs so nicely, and grinds her body into mine.

I take her hand and put it inside my jacket, she feels my paddle.

I say to her, "You are going to be spanked for leading this dance."

"Now, we have to stop this dance!"

I take her by the hand with me, over to my large desk. First I kiss her, then I say "You lie over this desk." "I want to see your ass, and give you your spanking for not following properly." "First I'll give you ten paddles."

After each stroke, I feel her ass gets warmer and redder.

"Now, tell me, how are you gonna dance next time?"

She says "The same way."

"Smart ass you are!"

"Ten more paddles, lover." "You don't know you are a follower yet do you?"

I give her ten more paddles, my cunt is getting wetter and wetter.

I slide my hands between her swollen lips and feel her clit.

My toy is rubbing between her ass.

"I am gonna fuck you in the ass."

She is moving her body with that dancing rhythm into me.

I say to her, "Will you behave next time we dance?"

"If so, I'll give you what you want now."

"Yes, yes," she says.

I touch and kiss her warm red ass. "Yes, I am gonna fuck my cha cha baby good."

She says, "I want you. Please, please, come inside me."

I turn her around, I kiss her, our lips, mouth, tongues are roughly, softly, passionately pressed together.

The lips are bitten and sucked.

I reach for her nipples and squeeze them. "Yes! Yes! More!" she says.

I turn her over on the desk.

I open her legs and rub her ass slowly as she writhes with her ass up I wet down my dildo. I gently rub the head of my dildo by her ass. She is so sexy. "You are such a good bad girl, I want to fuck you hard." I gently push my toy inside her ass and out slowly. Then I leave it still as she is squirming under me.

"Fuck! Fuck me baby! I want you harder" she says.

My cunt is throbbing. I want to go deeper into her. I push in and out of her harder and harder.

Her ass is slapping against the front of my legs.

She starts to swim in delight and groans loudly. I know she has come. I am so fuckin' hot for her to fuck me.

She reaches for me and puts her fingers and fist into my cunt.

I've wanted her so badly. It doesn't take long.

I come and gush out my juices all over her hand.

I am so full of wetness.

Our bodies are so moist and wet.

I take her to my bed and we hold one another.

I say to her, "Will you be my Cha Cha Cha Baby?"

Kitty Tsui

Phonesex

"HI. IT'S PAST MIDNIGHT HERE SO IT MUST BE after three your time. Did I wake you?"

"Ummmmm, yes... I was dozing. Can't really sleep, it's so hot and humid here. Thunderstormed earlier." Carley yawned and pushed the sheets away from her damp thighs. "I think I was dreaming about you."

"Oh? What?"

"Don't really remember. You were just here. When the phone rang it startled me. You're the only one who calls me this late. And I thought you were here in bed with me."

"Wish I were. Sorry I woke you."

"It's okay. You know I like it when you wake me."

"I have insomnia again. Don't know what's wrong with me but I hate it when I can't sleep. Wish I could come over and crawl into bed with you."

"Come on, then! How fast can you drive from San Francisco to New York City?" laughed Carley.

"If I borrow Mariko's beemer and break some speed records, maybe ten minutes. Can you wait that long?"

"Uh huh. Fifteen minutes max though. I'll even have tea and shortbread waiting for you when you get here."

"Tea and shortbread won't be the only things I'll want, darling."

"Oh? How hungry are you? Shall I fix a four course meal or will bacon and eggs do?"

"I'm hungry for you. Move over and let me get into bed with you. You are alone, aren't you?"

"I never sleep alone, dear, you should know that. There's a black and white fur ball in bed next to me."

"Well, have that fat cat move over 'cos I'm on my way. I'll have to dress in a hurry so I can get there in fifteen minutes. Don't have time to dress in full leather. What would you like to see me in?"

"Your black teddy will do just fine."

"Don't want to cause any accidents on the road. You know Mariko's car doesn't have tinted windows."

"Honey, it's dark and you'll be driving very fast. Who's going to see you? Okay, if you insist... hum, let me see. How about wearing your jeans and denim jacket over the teddy. They're easy to take off! Oh, and make sure they're your 501s."

"Certainly. Anything to oblige a lady! I'll even bring along my black leather gloves, safe sex supplies and a big tube of lube. Are you awake now?"

Carley laughed her deep, throaty laugh. "What do you think?"

"I think you're wide awake and already wet."

"Baby, I think you're right."

"Why don't you touch yourself and tell me how wet you are."

"I'm very wet. Come over, please. I can't wait fifteen minutes."

"You'll have to wait. You'll have to wait as long as I tell you to wait. What are you wearing?"

"Nothing. I just have black panties on."

"Take them off for me. Slowly. Hand them to me so I can smell you. Uummm. You smell great. You smell as good as I know you taste. What colour sheets are on your bed?"

"They're cream. With lace around the edges. I just bought them. Tonight's the first night I've slept on them."

"Really? Good. You know I love the feel of new sheets. Turn over on your stomach so I can see your ass. Put your arms up above your head and open your legs as wide as they'll go. I want to see you all stretched out on your new cream sheets. My hands are on your body, stroking the length of your neck, tracing the muscles along your back, kneading the curves of your thighs. I'm kissing the dimples in your ass." Mel paused. She could hear Carley's cries.

"Oh, Mel, oh, baby, I'm so hot for you. Oh, honey, please... oh baby, I want it all. I want as much as you can give me."

"I'm turned on too. I can feel myself wet through the denim."

"Baby, please fuck me, please."

"Not yet. You know you like it when I make you wait. Isn't that right?"

"Yes, baby, yes... oh, but I can't wait."

"Yes, yes you can. Yes you can, baby. I'm taking your ass in my mouth and biting you hard, running my tongue down your crack, licking both cheeks. I'm so turned on I can hardly wait to push inside you. I want to feel the whole force of my body inside you. Turn over and let me kiss you. Take my tongue inside you and suck on it. Oh yes, yes... your breasts are so full in my hands, your nipples so hard. I'm taking them in my mouth. I'm biting you."

"Oh God, Mel, I want to come."

"No, Carley, no. Not till I say so. I'm going to take you in my mouth, wrap my lips around your clitoris and suck on you."

"Ohhh, ohhh."

"My hands are on your nipples, my tongue licking your folds. Your juices are all over my mouth, you smell so good. I can't stop sucking on your clit. You taste so good and I want you so bad."

"Baby, I'm dripping wet for you."

"Good. I'm turned on too. I can feel my wetness through my blue jeans. Kiss me. Kiss me until I feel the distance between us closing and I'm in your bed with my legs wrapped around you."

"Yes, Mel, yes... I can feel you here. I can feel your hands and smell your heat."

"Do you want me, baby?"

"Honey, you know I do. I want all of you. I want as much as you can give me. I want you to push me really far. I want you to take me hard. I want to not think for a while, just feel. Please take me, honey. Fuck me, please."

"You're so hot and wet. My fingers are circling your clitoris, stroking your folds. I want to enter you with all my being. I want you to feel the power of my body moving inside you. Can you take it all?"

"Honey," Carley moaned, "please, yes... yes. I want to touch your body, your strong thighs in your tight jeans. I want to feel the muscles in your ass. I want your strong arms around me. I'm so hot for you, honey. Take me, please take me."

"You're dripping wet for me, baby. I want to push inside you with all the power in me. I want to penetrate you with my fingers. Can you feel me inside you? Two fingers... three, four. I want to slide my thumb inside your wetness. Relax, baby, open up to me. Let me rub your clitoris hard and fast. Feel my fingers enter you, curl and lodge inside your cunt in the place where fire is raging. My knuckles are straining to enter you. You know when I get excited I can't wait to push inside you. My mouth is on your mouth, my fingers squeezing your nipple, my fist lodged deep in your cunt. Do you feel me moving inside you?"

"Yes, honey, yes... oh, baby, don't stop. Please don't stop, baby."

"Give it to me, Carley, come for me. Give me everything you've got."

Mel could feel her power, the motion, her fist lodged inside her lover halfway up to the forearm. She could feel Carley's heat enveloping her fist and hear her cries of pleasure. Carley came to orgasm again and again and again in great spasms that gripped and rocked Mel's fist.

"I love you, baby," they echoed, in unison.

"Come lie in my arms," Mel whispered. "Come lie in my arms and let me hold you."

The fragrance of night-blooming jasmine drifted in through the open window into her bedroom. Mel could feel Carley's heartbeat on her breast as surely as she could feel the damp wetness in the crotch of her 501s.

Contributors' Notes

V.K. ARUNA lives and works in the Washington D.C. area. Writing fiction helps her "transcend" the barriers to physical travel; enabling her to return without leaving, to stay in touch when sounds and smells begin fading, to re-experience and re-imagine. She dedicates both pieces in this anthology to Yasmin Tambiah.

KAUSHALYA BANNERJI is a first generation Canadian writer. She has been published in *Diva: Literary Journal of South Asian Women, Fireweed: A Feminist Quarterly, Sami Yoni, The Toronto Review of Contemporary Writing Abroad, Canadian Woman Studies Journal,* and *Resources for Feminist Research/DRF.* Her writings have been anthologized in *Outrage: Dykes and Bis Resist Homophobia* (Women's Press, 1993) and in *A Lotus of Another Colour: An Unfolding of the South Asian Lesbian and Gay Experience* (Allyson Publications, 1992). She holds a master's degree in International Relations.

BILLY E. is a First Nations, Two-Spirited Metis from Manitoba living in Vancouver who is on her red road home to recording oral histories of her people. She is a heart talker and a spirit walker of our truths.

CAROL CAMPER is a Toronto-born writer, visual artist and women's health worker. Her writing has appeared in various anthologies and periodicals such as *Piece of my Heart: A Lesbian of Colour Anthology* and *Fireweed: A Feminist Quarterly*. She is creator and editor of *Miscegenation Blues: Voices of Mixed Race Women* (Sister Vision Press, 1994).

RITZ CHOW lives in Toronto, where she is currently studying at the University of Toronto and searching out her political feet. For now, she hopes her pair of Doc Martens will suffice.

CHRYSTOS was born November 7, 1946 in San Francisco of Menominee and European-immigrant parents. Self-Educated. Employed as a house-keeper. Her published books are *Not Vanishing, Dream On, In Her I Am,* (all published by Press Gang) and the forthcoming *Fugitive Colors,* Winner of the Cleveland State Poetry Center Audre Lorde Competition to be published by C.S.P.C. in May 1994.

CHERYL CLARKE is the author of four books of poetry. *Narratives: Poems in the Tradition of Black Women, Living as a Lesbian, Humid Pitch* and most recently, *Experimental Love.* She lives and works in New Jersey. She is perpetually interested in lesbian bodies as subjects of poetry.

ZAHRA DHANANI is a Khoji dyke who revels and finds nourishment in the beauty and spirit of her brown mothers/sisters/friends/lovers — so that on the side, she can kick `white-hetero-imperial-capito-phallo-patriarchal' Ass.

R.H. DOUGLAS is a Caribbean woman. The rhythms and sounds of the Caribbean run through her veins. She has been a poet, storyteller and consistent diarist for the past twenty years. She is an active member of the Harlem Writer's Guild and the International Women Writing Guild. Her work has been published in various anthologies.

JEWELLE GOMEZ lives in San Francisco, California, where she currently calls home. She has been an activist in movements against race, gender, class, and sexual oppression for over twenty years. She has published *Flamingoes and Bears,* a collection of poetry and *The Lipstick Papers.* Her first novel The Gilda Stories, was published by Firebrand Books in 1991. Her most recent book *Forty-Three Septembers* is a collection of essays which explore her writing experience as `Black Lesbian, Native American, raised poor, ex-catholic.... Firebrand Books, 1993.

MAXINE GREAVES is young, fresh, and has come out all over her sheets.

NAOMI GUILBERT is a biracial, bisexual, itinerant taiko player who lives, writes, and drums in Winnipeg, Manitoba and San Francisco, California.

EVE HARRIS is the pseudonym of a young woman in New York City. She divides her time between writing and loitering in nightclubs.

NICOLA HARWOOD is a dyke playwright, poet and performer who has been working in alternative and feminist theatre for ten years. Her solo show *Grrls Night Out* will premiere this year. She lives in Vancouver.

JENNY HEASMAN is a Londoner, she is 30 and of Anglo-Burmese descent. She is a lesbian feminist, living with her cat in a women's housing co-op overlooking Portobello Market. She can watch the Notting Hill Carnival from her living room. An avid reader of lonely heart ads, she likes to paint and write, and daydream about unspoilt countryside and lesbian utopias. She says she is a pretty average dyke-next-door.

TOMIYE ISHIDA is a mixed race Asian dyke, former whore, and survivor of life in general. She's still searching for home, but is currently stranded on Vancouver island where she does anti-discrimination work for an AIDS organization and writes whenever she can.

SALIMAH KASSIM-LAKHA is a twenty-something South Asian lesbian living in Toronto. She wants to be a star when she grows up.

L. LAI moves house a lot but is starting to feel at home in her Mount Pleasant apartment in Vancouver. A writer and a media activist, she has published poetry, fiction and articles in a number of anthologies and journals, and is a regular contributor to Kinesis. She is currently working on her first book. Born in the year of the sheep, she is not as quiet as she looks.

C. ALLYSON LEE has been published in *The Very Inside: An Anthology of Writing by Asian and Pacific Islander Lesbian and Bisexual Women, Outrage, West Coast Line, Piece of my Heart: A Lesbian of Colour Anthology, The Capilano Review, Fireweed: A Feminist Quarterly, Possibilitiis* and the *Journal for the Canadian Dental Association*. She has a smouldering passion for guitars, primates and WET Coast Womyn Warriors.

PATRICE LEUNG is so proud of her heritage that she cries when she watches shows on Chinese medicine, or hears the beat of a steel band. Joan Chen, however, provokes a different reaction.

LITTLE EARTHQUAKE. Brown, strong, womynloving South Asian-centric. Kali-worshipping passionate dyke in love with the erotic. She lives in Ontario.

MELO and MELIT are two Toronto dykes creating spaces and living and loving... many!

JUDITH NICHOLSON writes and survives daily in Montreal.

KALYANI H. PANDYA is a graduate student in English whose primary interest is in South Asian Canadian literature. A firm believer and disciplined practitioner of strategic daydreaming and a faithful disciple of the transformative properties of the imagination. Shares her life with feline companion Chelsea and human companion Ruth.

EFFIE POW was born in Malaysia, spent time with girls in double blue plaid in Toronto, lives in Vancouver by the ocean, and likes raspberry nipples.

MAKEDA SILVERA lives in Toronto, Canada. She is the author and anthologizer of several books which include: *Silenced, Growing Up Black, Remembering G and other stories, Her Head a Village and other stories, Piece of my Heart: A Lesbian of Colour Anthology*, and *The Other Woman: Women of Colour in Contemporary Canadian Literature*. She wants to write more erotica exploring themes of passion and obsession.

NATASHA SINGH is going to school part-time and working with Desh Pardesh, a festival held in Toronto annually that explores the politics of South Asian cultures in the West. She loves to write and is beginning to paint. She is a double pisces who is stuck on an aries — a lethal combination.

SHAHNAZ STRI was born in Bombay and came to Canada in 1976. She has been a poet since she was ten years old. She has been published in *Piece of my Heart: A Lesbian of Colour Anthology* and *Fireweed: A Feminist Quarterly* and is working on a collection of poetry and prose.

LISA VALENCIA-SVENSSON is a half-breed Filipina-Canadian dyke. She especially enjoys savouring poems about eating juicy/sweet/ripe mangoes, although other fruits can work well too.

SHERECE TAFFE is a woman-identified woman who spends most of her time raising her three-year-old daughter — Sharmylae Tjonda — and aspiring to be her true goddess self. She lives in Ontario.

KITTY TSUI is the author of *The Words of a Woman Who Breathes Fire*. She is at work on her first novel and a book of erotic short stories entitled *"Breathless."*

N. SC. WOO is a Chinese-Canadian who stares longingly at the moon waiting for a transcontinental connection. She likes to live by profound mottos such as the one on her obento box: "Don't just say, `ribbit' — Live it!"